MINE TO HOLD

SAFE HARBOR SERIES

JEN TALTY

JUPITER PRESS

PRAISE FOR JEN TALTY

"Deadly Secrets is the best of romance and suspense in one hot read!" *NYT Bestselling Author Jennifer Probst*

"A charming setting and a steamy couple heat up the pages in a suspenseful story I couldn't put down!" *NY Times and USA today Bestselling Author Donna Grant*

"Jen Talty's books will grab your attention and pull you into a world of relatable characters, strong personalities, humor, and believable storylines. You'll laugh, you'll cry, and you'll rush to get the next book she releases!" Natalie Ann USA Today Bestselling Author

"I positively loved *In Two Weeks*, and highly recommend it. The writing is wonderful, the story is fantastic, and the characters will keep you coming back for more. I can't wait to get my hands on future installments of the NYS Troopers series." *Long and Short Reviews*

"*In Two Weeks* hooks the reader from page one. This is a fast paced story where the development of the romance grabs you emotionally and the suspense keeps you sitting on the edge of your chair. Great characters, great writing, and a believable plot that can be a warning to all of us." *Desiree Holt, USA Today Bestseller*

"*Dark Water* delivers an engaging portrait of wounded hearts as the memorable characters take you on a healing journey of love. A mysterious death brings danger and intrigue into the drama, while sultry passions brew into a believable plot that melts the reader's heart. Jen Talty pens an entertaining romance that grips the heart as the colorful and dangerous story unfolds into a chilling ending." *Night Owl Reviews*

"This is not the typical love story, nor is it the typical mystery. The characters are well rounded and interesting." *You Gotta Read Reviews*

"*Murder in Paradise Bay* is a fast-paced romantic thriller with plenty of twists and turns to keep you guessing until the end. You won't want to miss this one..." *USA Today bestselling author Janice Maynard*

Everyone needs a safe harbor to sail into. Prepare to be captivated by a story that will keep you on the edge of your seat until the final, shocking climax.

In the seaside town of Lighthouse Cove, Deputy Sheriff Emmerson Kirby thought he had seen it all. But everything changes when a mysterious stranger named Rumor Crimson enters his life. Rumor, with her striking emerald eyes and enigmatic past, is thrust into the center of a crime that shakes the foundations of the tight-knit community.

As Emmerson investigates a series of baffling murders, he becomes convinced that Rumor holds the key to unraveling the truth. But with each step closer to the dark secrets that haunts the small town, Emmerson finds himself drawn deeper into a web of deceit, betrayal, and danger. Rumor, meanwhile, must confront her own demons and face the consequences of her past.

Together, Emmerson and Rumor navigate a treacherous path and their lives intertwine in unexpected ways. As they race against time to expose the sinister forces at play, they discover that trust can be shattered in an instant, and that the line between ally and enemy is blurred.

In this gripping tale of love, suspense, and redemption, Emmerson and Rumor must confront their darkest fears and fight against the odds. Will they uncover the truth before it's too late? Or will the secrets buried in Lighthouse Cove consume them both?

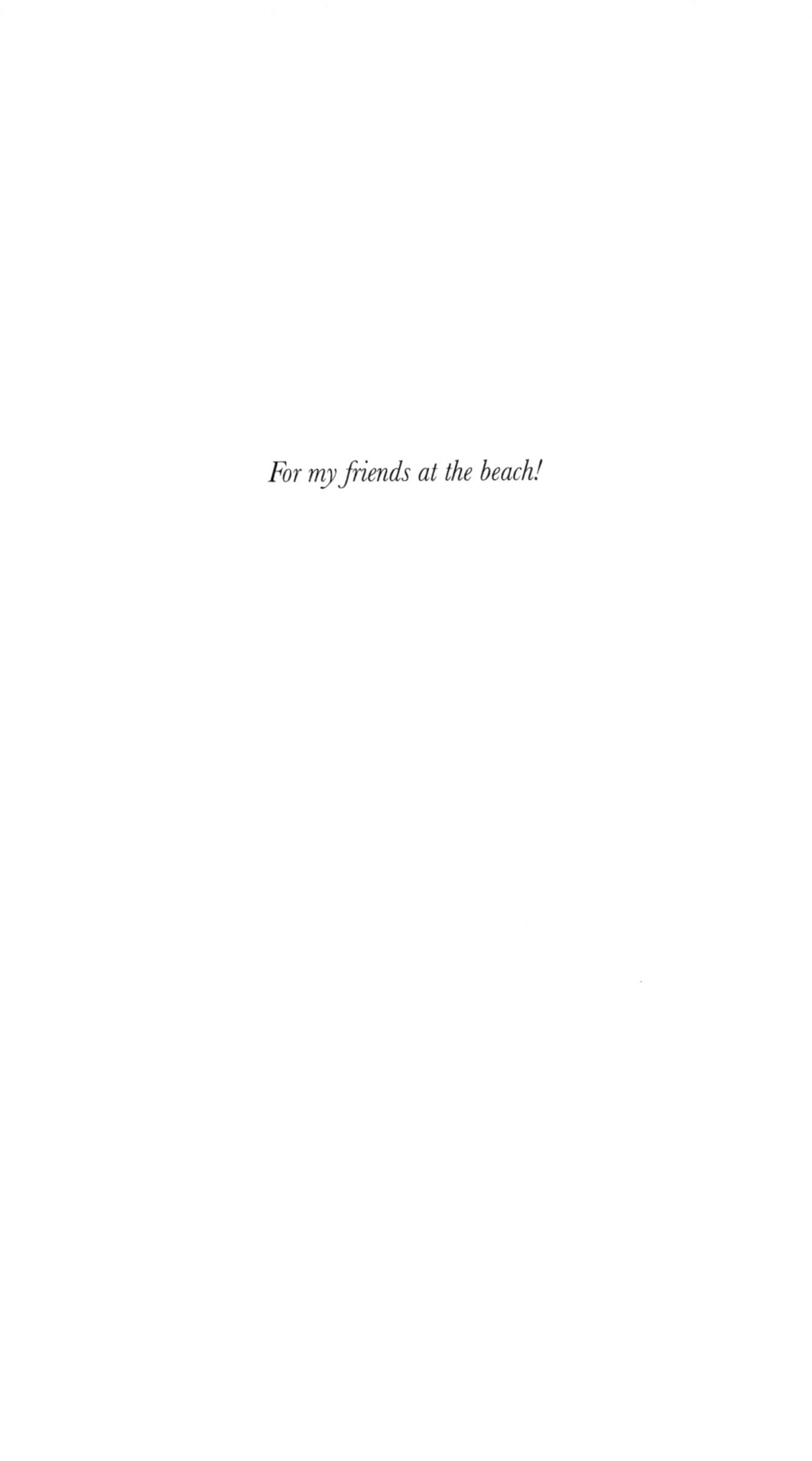

For my friends at the beach!

FIFTEEN YEARS AGO...

The smell of death filled Rumor Crimson's nostrils. It reminded her of three-day old fish mixed with sour milk. It was a scent she wouldn't soon forget. It clung to her throat and imprinted on her brain.

She blinked but couldn't look away from the dead body. She hadn't killed the man, but his blood was on her hands.

Tony, her boyfriend, with plastic gloves on his hands, lifted the dead man's cell. He tapped the screen. "Oh my God. Help. Help. There's a gunman in—" Tony dropped the phone to the floor.

"What are you doing?" she whispered.

Tony wiped the sweat from his brow with his bloodstained T-shirt. "When people steal from the boss, lie about it, and then try to run, this is what happens."

She swallowed. In the four months she and Tony had been out of foster care and on their own, her life had turned into a living hell. Worse than being abused and abandoned by her biological parents.

Worse than the system fucking her in the ass.

She'd trusted Tony and thought she loved him, but what a mistake it had been to follow him through life. He was nothing but a loser and a criminal.

And now, a murderer.

"Not what I was talking about, and you steal from Tom."

Tony raised his arm. The back of his hand landed on her cheek with a thud and a crack.

Her head snapped.

A sharp pain shot through her system like a lightning bolt.

She groaned. "That wasn't necessary." She wiped the blood that trickled from her face. It wasn't the first time he'd hit her. But it sure as shit was going to be the last.

"Don't fucking talk back to me, bitch. You don't know shit. Now, go get the drugs. I'll carry the money. We have to roll. The cops will be here in ten minutes."

"I can't do this anymore," she whispered.

He grabbed her by the hair and yanked. "You and me, babe. We're in this now, together."

"I told you I didn't want to be part of the drug

business. You can do whatever you want, but when I moved in with you, I said—"

"Shut up." He gave her a good shove.

She stumbled backward, nearly tripping over the dead body. Bile smacked the back of her throat like a rocket launch. She'd do this one last thing, and then she'd run. She had no idea where she'd go, but she was done. Tony wasn't the man she thought he was and she sure as shit wasn't cut out for this kind of life. She hadn't endured years of suffering to end up in a cell.

Turning on her heel, she raced off toward the kitchen and dumped the cocaine into the duffel bag and quickly followed Tony out of the apartment.

"Get in the car," Tony commanded.

She sank into the front seat. Tears burned the corners of her eyes. But she wouldn't cry. Not now. Not in front of him.

Sirens blared. Two cop cars came charging out of nowhere from the other direction. This was it. She was going to be arrested as an accomplice to murder.

During her short life, she'd learned to distrust cops and most authority figures. They never did what they said they were going to do. She'd been pushed around from one foster family to the next since she'd been eleven.

That was after two cops came into her home and took her away.

Of course, she'd been living alone for six weeks.

Even she knew that was wrong, but she still resented the way the police had gone about yanking her from the only home she'd ever known.

She glanced over her shoulder as the police cars sped by, completely ignoring them.

Tony smiled. "All part of the plan."

"Why are we going home? Why aren't you going to Tom's?" She shifted her gaze.

"Mind your own business."

This wasn't good. She'd been sitting right next to Tony when the call came in.

Go get my product, my money, and bring it to me.

Was Tony going to really double-cross Tom? Not a good idea.

"When you kill a man in front of me and expect me to go along, it is my business. Now tell me what you plan on doing?"

"It's pretty simple." Tony snagged his phone and tapped the screen. It rang twice.

"Tony, man. What's the good news," Tom's voice bellowed through the vehicle.

"Shit, dude. You're not going to like this one bit. But I just circled Ollie's building and had to bug out. The cops are there. I don't know why, but it's not looking good."

"Don't fuck with me, Tony. I'm not in the mood."

"Dude, I'm not," Tony said. "I'll go back in an hour when things calm down."

"You better. And you better keep me posted. I'm sick of that little shit stealing from me. Deal with this, or I'm dealing with you."

"Yes, sir."

The line went dead.

Tony was going to be dead too, if he wasn't careful.

She had no intentions of letting that be her fate.

As soon as Tony pulled into the parking lot of their shitty-ass apartment where the halls had a constant stench of weed, she snagged the bag of cocaine and hauled ass inside.

Tony cracked open a beer, opened a bottle of pills, and washed them down with a big gulp.

"Want one, babe?" he asked.

"You know I don't do that shit." She'd tried it once and she fucking hated it.

"You should take one. Or two. It will help calm you down." He took his beer and flopped on the pullout sofa, which was also their bed. He flicked on the television. Something he stole and he was so freaking proud of that. "Holy shit." He leaned forward, pointing frantically. "They're already reporting on Ollie."

"A man was shot and killed today in the building behind me. Police have not made any statements yet. However, we do know that the victim has an extensive record. He served time for drug trafficking and was released from prison two years ago. We'll report back more at six."

"That's fucking perfect," Tony said. "Do you have any idea how much money is in that bag over there?"

"I don't."

"Fifty grand. In unmarked bills." He smiled. "And the coke? That's worth a lot. I cut it right, we can make a killing and Tom will think one of his enemies killed Ollie for it. We're set." He leaned back again, tucking a hand inside his pants.

Tom wasn't the kind of man you crossed and she wasn't going to be around when Tony figured that out.

"I need a shower." She palmed her cheek. It still throbbed.

"When you're done, make me a sandwich."

"Sure." She grabbed a change of clothes and padded to the small bathroom that looked as though it had never been cleaned. She turned the water on as hot as it would go and stripped.

Standing under the lukewarm water, she let the tears flow. She and Tony had such big plans. They were going to prove their foster parents wrong. That Tony wasn't a bad kid. He wasn't going to wind up a loser. He was going to clean up. He promised to quit smoking pot. He was going to go to college. Get a job.

And so was she.

They were going to have a sweet life together.

But one month out of foster care, Tony was running drugs.

He said it was temporary, just to get them some quick cash so they could follow their dreams. He wasn't making enough at the auto repair shop and her job as a waitress wasn't bringing in much either.

Once again, she believed him because she thought she loved him.

But this wasn't love.

And nothing had changed.

He was the same idiot she'd met two years ago when he landed in foster care. His sob story about his life, though real, was the crutch he used to stay the same.

Quickly, she dried off with the stained towel that smelled like mildew. Her clothes came from the Goodwill store down the street. She hiked her over-sized jeans up and pulled her shirt over her head.

When she stepped out of the bathroom, Tony was sound asleep on the sofa.

Thank God.

It was now or never.

Quietly, she snagged the bag of cash, her purse with her phone in it, and slipped out the door. As soon as she got to the corner, she got out her cell and called 9-1-1.

"What is your emergency?"

"I know someone who has a big bag of cocaine in his apartment. The address is 80 E 113 Street in the Watts neighborhood. I believe he's armed."

"What's your name, ma'am. Are you there? And are you safe?"

"I'm not there, and yes. I'm safe. But hurry. Please. I think he might have had something to do with the murder of that man earlier today in Hollywood." Rumor ended the call. She turned off her cell, dropped it to the pavement, and crushed it with her cowboy boots. Bending over, she lifted the busted electronic equipment and tossed it in the trash.

Hoisting the heavy bag of cash over her shoulder, she walked as quickly as she could—without drawing attention to herself—toward the bus stop. She ducked into a convenience store for a soda and some change. She didn't want any paper trail.

She had no idea where she'd go. Alaska? Montana? Maybe Utah? Some place where it snowed. She hated cold weather and Tony would never look for her in one of those places.

She would leave California, and she'd never come back. Ever.

Sitting on the park bench, two police cars rolled by.

She clutched the bag.

The cops kept going.

Hopefully, to go arrest Tony.

The bus came a few minutes later. She climbed aboard, dropping her coins, and asked the driver for a transfer. It would take a good hour and a half to two hours to get to the Greyhound station. The only decision then would be what ticket she would buy.

She didn't care.

First one out of town that got her the farthest distance.

Time to really start her life over.

1

Emmerson Kirby lifted the family's newest addition and pressed his lips against her chubby cheeks. He blew a big fat raspberry. God, he loved babies. They smelled like innocence and looked at you like you had all the answers.

Six-month-old Siggy laughed. And laughed. This wild belly laugh filled his heart and soul with more love than he knew what to do with.

Damn, his brother's little girl had stolen his heart.

All his nieces and nephews had done that.

And he didn't play favorites, but Siggy was his goddaughter and he'd developed a special bond with her.

"You're too stinking cute." He kissed her nose. "And you are stinky. But Uncle Emmerson doesn't do dirty diapers. Not even for you." He handed Siggy back to Rhett. "She's all yours, man."

"You know, her uncle Chris does diaper duty." Rhett waved to Shelby, pointing to the little girl in his lap, who chewed on his thumb. "And I seem to remember you changing all of Seth and Nathan's kids when they were little."

"I was young and stupid. Now I'm old and have learned to give them back to their parents." Emmerson smiled.

Shelby stood by the deep end of his mother and stepfather's pool. It was still strange to call Steve his stepfather, but it made his mother insanely happy, so he went with it.

But what was weirder was the fact that Steve was his little brother's biological father. Jameson didn't call Steve *Dad*. At least not most of the time. The few times it slipped out, no one said a word about it. Not even his mother. But everyone caught the emotion laced in her tearful eyes.

Jameson had no idea Steve was his father until a few years ago and it rocked the very foundation of the Kirby family. Jameson still refused his mother's wish to take Steve's name and he never would.

Steve had told Jameson that while he'd love nothing more, he respected and valued the man who had raised him and preferred Jameson to keep the family name. The ones his brothers had.

And that was the name he'd given his children.

Today, things were steady as she goes.

"Besides, you're pawning her off on your wife." Emmerson laughed.

"She has the diaper bag and the breasts that feed this kid. In about ten minutes, she'll be screaming bloody murder, and my boobs don't produce milk."

"You do have nice breasts." Emmerson reached out and massaged his brother's pec. "You filled out that dress real nice."

"You're an asshole." Rhett batted his hand away.

"How's my little princess?" Shelby lifted Siggy out of Rhett's lap, before leaning over and kissing her husband. "Why the sourpuss face?"

"I'm never going to live down putting on that damn dress for you. Why did you have to go and show my family? That was just mean."

Shelby hiked the little girl on her hip. "Not mean. Funny as hell and I swear, you looked better in that bridesmaid dress than I did."

"That's the last time I do a favor like that. Besides, it was a joke and only meant for you and me." Rhett shook his head. "Next time, I'll lay the dress on the bed with the jewelry and shoes to see how they look."

"I still can't believe you put it on." Shelby ran her fingers through Rhett's long hair. "Can't wait to see you play dress-up with this one."

"This next one better be a boy," Rhett muttered. "I need some testosterone in my home."

"Next one?" Emmerson arched a brow. "Why, Shelby, are you pregnant already?"

"I'm not getting any younger, and my brother's still butt hurt over you being this one's godfather. We had to have another one." Shelby laughed. "Besides, your brother has it in his head he wants four kids." She wiggled her fingers. "But that ain't happening. I'm too old for that shit. Depending on how this pregnancy goes, I might give him a third, but that's a big might."

"Congratulations. I'm really happy for both of you. Now with the woman carrying Trinity and Emmett's little one, it will have a cousin about the same age to play with. I love that." Emmerson was one of seven boys. Of the seven, five were married with kids and the pressure of him and Miles to settle down and get married was astronomical.

And not just from his mother, who was relentless.

But his father, his stepfather, his siblings, and their wives had all joined in. Even his fourteen- and eleven-year-old nephews had tried setting him up. He could find his own dates. Although, at forty-two, he was stuck in his ways and finding a woman to put up with his quirks was becoming a chore he didn't enjoy.

He wasn't unhappy with his life. He loved his career as a police officer and detective for the Lighthouse Cove Police Department. Sometimes working for his mother could be a royal pain in the ass and he couldn't wait for her to retire.

She threatened to all the time, but never did.

But when that happened, he'd end up working for

his brother, Nathan. That wouldn't be so bad. They had similar opinions and butted heads a lot less.

"Thanks," Shelby said. "I better go get this little sweetie changed and fed so I can put her down for a nap." She turned on her heel and strolled toward the sliding glass doors that led to the massive kitchen.

Emmerson's mother was loaded. Well, she wasn't, but her husband had millions. Emmerson had no idea how much, but the house—if he were to sell it—could get him at least twenty million.

It had to be the finest piece of property in all of Lighthouse Cove, Florida.

He turned his head and stared out toward the ocean. It was a good walk to get there and he could barely see the sand. But he could see the pretty blue waves rolling in. It was rare that the entire family could ever get together, so it was nice to see all his brothers in one place.

Jameson was in the pool with his two kids. Nathan was with him, while his two older kids splashed and played with some of their younger cousins.

Their wives huddled on lounge chairs, deep in conversation.

Emmett and Miles were leaning against the bar, staring up at the baseball game on the television.

Trinity, Emmett's wife, looped her arm around her husband, watching, acting as if she cared. She was good that way, but Emmerson also knew this was the second time they were trying to adopt a baby. The first birth mother backed out two months into the process and Trinity was beyond nervous the second time.

Seth sat on the edge of the pool next to their father, the two lawyers in the family. His wife and Emmerson's mother were somewhere in the house.

His mom had taken to being wealthy better than anyone could have expected. She'd been frugal his entire childhood. Now, she spent like she had deep pockets and didn't have a care in the world.

Okay, not entirely true, but she didn't worry anymore.

And she'd catered the family party.

Three waitresses strolled around with trays, one of which had more than caught his attention, but only because he'd seen her twice in town in the last three days.

There was one bartender. A chef to man the grill. And a chef inside.

Afterward, his mom would have a cleaning service.

But all this made his mother happy, something she hadn't been the last few years she'd been married to his father, and the first year Steve had come back into her life.

The waitress, Rumor, the one he hadn't been able to keep his eyes off, strolled by. "Would you boys like a couple of cheeseburger sliders?" She leaned over, holding the tray close to the table. "They're fresh. Just got them from the chef."

"They smell delicious." Emmerson took the small plate she offered and snagged three. "Thanks," he said. "Aren't you the girl who served me breakfast yesterday? Rumor, is it?"

"That's me." She gave him the same bright smile she had when she'd served him in the Safe Harbor Café. "You commented on my name being the same as Bruce Willis' daughter."

Emmerson waggled his finger. "And you told me you were named after the Fleetwood Mac album."

"Glad you remember the conversation." Her long dark hair was pulled back at the nape of her neck in a messy bun. She wore a standard white button-down blouse, but he could see a tattoo peeking out from her wrist. He didn't know what it was, but it intrigued him.

She intrigued him.

Her eyes were the color of a bright shiny emerald. It was an intoxicating look and he found himself star- ing. Her complexion was fair, but it had been kissed by the sun.

There was something about this girl that had crawled under his skin. He'd gone back to Safe Harbor Café this morning, but she hadn't been there. He'd gone as far as to inquire about her with the owners, Lucy Ann and Phil. They informed him that she had just started working, but his mother snatched her up for this party.

Lucy Ann and Phil would do anything for his mother, including releasing one or two of their staff when his mom and Steve catered a party.

"You are definitely memorable and it's good to see you again," Emmerson said. "Have you met my brother, Rhett?"

"Not officially, but isn't everyone here a brother? When your mom was briefing me for the job, she said she has seven sons."

Rhett laughed. "I think she kept trying for a girl and finally gave up after Jameson was born, but yeah, we're all brothers."

"The family resemblance is a little disturbing." She stood taller. "Can I get you anything else? Fresh beers?"

"We can get those on our own," Emmerson said.

"That's what I'm here for." She nodded. "I'll be right back."

He cocked his head as she walked away, her hips swaying in her black shorts. He sucked in a deep breath and let it slowly.

"Stare much?" Rhett asked.

"Just trying to make out the tattoo on her ankle." So far, Emmerson had counted four tats. Three on her ankles, and the one on her wrist. He couldn't help but wonder if there were more.

And he wasn't a tattoo man.

Even if he did have one.

"Watch this, Uncle Emmerson. Uncle Rhett," Ally, Seth's youngest, yelled from the diving board. She ran toward the end and flipped.

When she popped up, Emmerson stuck his thumb and finger between his lips, whistling loudly. "Woot. Woot. That's a ten."

"Great job, kiddo." Rhett gave her a thumbs-up.

"This family's pumping out babies like it's hurricane season." Emmerson lifted his beer and swigged. "Ten and counting."

Rhett laughed. "Now you're changing the subject."

"From what?"

"The cute chick who served you the cheeseburgers." Rhett reached over and snatched one up, plopping it in his mouth. "I've been watching you eye her all day."

"I have not." Emmerson nibbled on one of the burgers. He'd been eating all day but kept missing the trays that Rumor had been passing around. All he wanted was five minutes to say hello.

"Then how did you know she had tats, because I didn't until you pointed them out." Rhett cocked his head.

"I'm curious about the new person in town. She's working at Safe Harbor Café and I spend a lot of time there."

"Is she now." Rhett cocked a brow before lifting

his beer. "What else have you found out about… what's her name?"

"Rumor and nothing, really. Other than she moved to town last week and she asked Lucy Ann about affordable short-term rentals in the area." Emmerson rubbed his jaw.

"You're seriously not thinking about renting her your pool house, are you?"

"I was going to list it anyway."

"No. You talked about it, and you keep changing your mind, stating you're not sure you want a stranger living that close, using your backyard and all the hassles that go with being a landlord."

"Yeah, but sometimes things fall in your lap."

"Oh my God. I think you want her to fall in your lap."

"Shut the fuck up." Emmerson took a napkin and tossed it at his brother. "She's too young."

"How old do you think she is?"

"I know she's thirty-three."

"How the hell do you know that?" Rhett asked.

"Lucy Ann told me." Emmerson cringed. "And before you go reading too much into that, I was only asking because that's when I got the idea I might rent to her. Lucy Ann said Rumor had mentioned she had looked at a few places, but they were all out of her price range. Lucy Ann thinks this girl might be down on her luck. Or maybe going through a tough time.

Either way, my pool house is basically a studio. It's only about four hundred square feet, which is tiny."

"Yeah. But it's on the fucking water. Right in your backyard, facing your brand-new million-dollar home, with new pool and all the perks that go with living in an upscale neighborhood. You could get top dollar, even if it is small."

"Why do you care if I rent it out or not?"

Rhett chuckled. "I don't. But I've only seen that look in your eyes a couple of times. First time was with—"

"Don't you dare bring her up," Emmerson said behind a tight jaw. He lifted the last burger and shoved it in his mouth. He couldn't believe Edwina had moved back to Lighthouse Cove. It was like pouring salt on an open wound.

Worse, she fucking flirted with him like she hadn't ripped his heart out and stomped on it with her three-inch heels.

"Fucking woman is making me crazy." Emmerson lifted his beer and finished the last drop.

Rumor strolled across the pool patio with two fresh beers.

He locked gazes with her. It settled his nerves, but it amped up other emotions, something he wasn't prepared for nor expected. Being attracted to a person didn't mean anything.

But now he wanted to act.

He needed to tread lightly.

"Here you go, boys." She set the drinks on the table. "If you need anything else, just let me know."

"Will do. Thanks." Emmerson smiled.

She went about making her rounds with the rest of the family. What a nice cushy job and her mother would pay really well. That should help her get her feet on the ground.

Rhett leaned forward, resting his arms on the table. "Look. I know Edwina is a sore subject. I get it. I was there. I know what she did. I also know that you have no love in your heart for her."

"When she came back, Mom was terrified I would somehow magically forgive Edwina." Emmerson chuckled. "Funny things is, I have. When I first saw her, there wasn't even a pang of hatred or resentment. There was nothing. It was like when you read a book and it's neither great nor horrible. It's a shrug of the shoulders, and then you forget it, never to think of it again."

"I get that," Rhett said. "But you loved her once."

"A really long time ago."

"I have to ask. What has you so pissed off now?"

Emmerson hadn't told anyone about Edwina's antics. Why bother. She'd give up, eventually. Hopefully. He reached across the table and turned his cell over, tapping the screen, finding the texts. "You can read them for yourself, noting I only responded to the first one, telling her that I wished her well, but I would not be taking her out, ever again."

"As in on a date? A romantic one?" Rhett held the phone in his hand with an arched brow. "You've got to be kidding me. After what she did? She's lucky she didn't go to jail, thanks to you and Mom."

"And I'm lucky I don't have half a dozen sexually transmitted diseases." Emmerson let out a long breath. Talk about being made a fool of. His fiancée had been a madam. She'd been doing it right under his nose. Him. A cop. His mother, the chief of police.

What a shit show that had been.

"She left town eighteen years ago, and she's sending you texts like this?" Rhett tapped the screen. *"Hey, Emmerson. Meet me for a drink? Like old times? I've missed you. I want to catch up. Make up for all the mistakes. Start fresh."*

"It gets worse. In one of the texts she talks about how compatible we once were in bed. She went into a little too much detail."

"She's a fucking whack job." Rhett set the phone on the table. "Do you think she's changed?"

Emmerson nodded. "I didn't do this because I'm even remotely interested. I did it for the safety of young college students and bored housewives in town. I had one of Mom's contacts with the FBI do a full background on Edwina. She's clean. When she left here, she finished her degree and has been working in finance ever since. She landed a job with a local car dealership as their finance manager."

"How you and Mom managed to keep what she'd been doing a secret is beyond me."

"People know and they whisper, but that's not the point. I don't know if this falls under the category of good news or not, but Edwina had only been involved in the sex trafficking ring for six months. She gave Mom details, names, dates. Enough to bust the ring. Mom got the ADA to cut her a deal and she walked. Probably more so out of respect for me and my situation. But at the end of the day, I'm glad for her sake she put it behind her."

"Yeah, but to think you'd take her back after that kind of betrayal and almost twenty years, that's just fucking crazy talk."

"I really don't know if that's what she wants."

"I just read the texts, man. That's what it looks like to me and she hasn't let go of that history."

"There's a big part of me that isn't sure that at twenty I even knew what love was. I thought I did and I gave Edwina two years of my life. Looking back, I think I loved the idea of her. But I was young and stupid. I look at our life growing up. Being one of seven, as nuts as it was at times, was fantastic. I thought I wanted all that."

"Are you saying you don't want a family at all now?"

"I'm almost forty-three years old. I think that ship has sailed."

"Jesus Christ. Have you forgotten you're talking to your *older* brother. I'm forty-five. My wife is in her early forties. We're seven months away from having a second child." He jerked his head toward Rumor, who leaned against the bar, tugging at her bun. "The reason I brought up Edwina is she's the first woman to put that spark of life in your eyes." He held up his hand. "Since then, outside of Tessa, all you've had are a string of one-night stands, short romances—"

"I'm not a dirty dog."

"I'm not saying you are," Rhett said. "But in the last eighteen years you've had maybe three real relationships. Ones where we all thought you might have learned to trust again and be vulnerable. But as soon as the shit got real, you got out. Didn't matter that your eyes danced with the promise of something bigger, you chose to let fear rule you. You and I shared that trait."

Emmerson wouldn't deny that fact. "Okay. I hear you. Edwina fucked with my head." He shrugged. "I have serious trust issues with women. Outside of Seth and Nathan, we all did, thanks to Mom or some other chick who broke our hearts and trust. What does that have to do with Rumor or me renting my pool house to her?"

"We are our mother's sons and we jump in with

two feet and our eyes closed and I can already see the writing on the wall."

"I'm not interested in Rumor like that. I don't even know her. Besides, she's too young."

"That's an excuse you're trying to sell yourself. It's not a big deal and trust me, little brother. I'm not blind. I've been sitting here with you for the last hour and you can't take your eyes off her."

Emmerson didn't have the energy to argue. Rhett was right. Emmerson wanted to get to know Rumor. He wanted to know what possessed her to get tattoos. What they meant. Were they special? Why did she move to Lighthouse Cove? What was her history?

He had a million questions and they had plagued him all night.

"I'll admit she's gorgeous and there's something about her that has held my curiosity for more than five seconds. But you know me, I don't act until I know more. Not unless I'm being a dog." He arched a brow.

"I doubt she's the type of girl who does one-night stands." Rhett laughed. "Look. You always overthink things. You're the cop, I'm the private dick. So let me do what I do best. I'll do the background check for the pool house. I'll do a little research into her past. If there are any red flags, I'll bring them to you. Otherwise, I'll keep what I find to myself."

Emmerson arched a brow. "I don't like you knowing more about her than I do."

"The point is for you to get to know her the old-fashioned way. You know, take her out on a date. Ask questions. Tell her things about yourself. If at any point you really feel the need to see what I've learned, we can talk. But if you do it up front, you'll never go out with her to begin with, because if she even has one unpaid parking ticket, you'll run for the fucking hills."

Emmerson shifted his gaze. Rumor had moved from the bar, carrying another tray, this time filled with shrimp on a stick. She stopped briefly to admire Axel, Nathan's one-year-old, and his new toy truck. It had been six months since Emmerson had been out on a real date. Two years since he had a girlfriend who lasted more than a month. He didn't consider himself a lonely man. He was content in his life. He had friends, and he had his family.

But he had to admit, having a companion to share his life with would be nice. But his track record with women had to be the worst.

Although, if he were being honest, he hadn't given anyone a real chance since Tessa and that was ten years ago.

"What do you say, little brother? Are you going to ask out Rumor and let me do the digging?"

"Yeah." He took his beer and stood.

"You're going to do this now? At Mom's party?"

He stared at his big brother and lowered his chin. "Mother has already been on me to ask her out."

"You asshole. You let me give that speech and you were going to do it anyway?"

Emmerson shrugged. "With Mom, it felt more like I was doing it for her." He squeezed Rhett's shoulder. "At least your little pep talk had my best interests at heart and wasn't all about my sperm and the Kirby last name."

2

"I'm sorry to have kept you so late."

"It's no problem," Rumor said with a big smile. When she accepted this job, she'd been told that the chief of police didn't just tip well. That if Rumor went above and beyond, she'd get a thick wad of cash and Rumor needed it. She'd spent more on the used vehicle she just bought than she'd wanted to, but she loved the damn car.

And it was reliable. She'd get years out of it, and with the amount of miles she would wind up putting on it, she was glad to make the investment.

"I hope you don't mind getting paid in cash." Rebecca Jayne handed her a thick envelope. "I added the extra hour, and there's a sizable tip."

"You didn't have to do that." She stuffed the envelope in her back pocket with her heart beating wildly in her throat. It wasn't a tickle. It was a big *thump,*

thump, thump that made her wonder if she suddenly grew an Adam's apple.

"Oh, yes, I did," Rebecca said. "You're a hard worker, and my family kept you jumping all afternoon. I want to hire you for more events, if that's okay with you."

"Absolutely." Rumor nodded. "I'd love that."

"Good. Now, please. Take off that apron, change into your bathing suit, and enjoy yourself."

"Oh. No. I couldn't do that." She shook her head, glancing around.

"You can, and I insist. If you didn't bring a suit, I have plenty. Just go over to the pool house and pick one out." Rebecca squeezed her forearm. "I would be very upset if you didn't stay for a bit. I worked you to the bone."

Steve, her husband, approached, wrapping his arm around Rebecca's waist. He was a tall man and didn't look anything like anyone else in the room.

Except Jameson. They had some similarities and Rumor had learned Steve was Jameson's father.

But no one else's.

Interesting.

God, she loved small-town life sometimes. As long as she wasn't the center of attention.

"Honey, the chef needs you for a moment," Steve said.

"Okay." Rebecca smiled. "Don't you dare leave

without at least dipping your feet into the pool or enjoying some of the food. You deserve it."

Rumor untied her apron and set it behind the bar. She untucked her shirt and unbuttoned it, showing off her bikini top. Rebecca had made it clear from the beginning that everyone who worked her parties was expected to enjoy themselves when their work was done.

She glanced around, eyeing the handsome police officer, Emmerson, with two *M*'s. What a strange way to spell the name. Then again, her parents had named her Rumor, so who was she talk?

Emmerson stood approximately ten feet away, chatting with one of his brothers. Emmett maybe. Another cop.

So many law enforcement people around made her want to jump in her car and drive off—at the speed limit, of course. No matter how many years she put between her and her past, she still worried that Tony, if he ever got out of prison, or worse, Tom, would get ahold of her.

She'd be dead for sure.

Snagging a soda, because she didn't dare take an adult beverage, she decided she'd at least sit at the edge of the pool and soak in a few rays. A half hour. That was it.

"Hey, Rumor." Emmerson stopped her before she made it across the pool deck. "I see my mom finally let you off the hook." He stood there with his button-down shirt open, while his ripped abs taunted her eyes. He had blondish hair, cut short, but too short. His dark eyes danced in the sun's rays.

She wasn't very good at guessing people's ages, but she gathered he was somewhere around forty based on the rest of his brothers.

Emmerson had a quiet personality. Most of the Kirby brothers did, even at their own party. While they had engaging conversations, laughed loudly, and played hard with the kids, she could tell they were a reserved bunch with a slightly twisted sense of humor.

"I've been released but told I must check out the pool before I leave and I wouldn't want to insult your mother. She's been very good to me."

"She has her moments." He took her soda from her hands. "Let's get you something stronger. A beer perhaps? Or maybe you're a wine girl?"

"I like wine, but I'm more of a whiskey drinker." She laughed nervously. "However, I'm at a party filled with cops. Not a good idea to have a drink and then get in my car."

"One drink won't impair you, especially if you sip it and don't leave for an hour." He pressed his hand on her lower back, guiding her back toward the bar. "Do you like beer?"

She wanted to dig her heels in and protest. But this was the host's son. "I do and I'll have one. But then I really do have to go."

"Big plans?" He reached behind the bar, grabbing two bottles. He twisted off the caps, handing her one.

"I've got a hot date with a rental app. The place I'm staying at now needs me out in three days."

"That's not enough time to find a place."

"It's an Airbnb and even if they could extend it, I don't want to, so I'm hoping this little town with the tagline, *Everyone needs a safe harbor to sail into*, will find me something else quickly."

He waved his hand. "Let's go take a walk on the beach."

She cocked her head.

He chuckled. "I'm a cop, not a serial killer."

"The last book I read, the FBI agent was the bad guy and a super creeper. Like gave me nightmares creepy, so it happens."

"That's true, but it's a beautiful night. The ocean is calm. There's a light breeze, and my mother might have put the bug in my ear that I should show you her private beach." He raised his elbow. "It will also give me the chance to tell you about a great little pool house for rent that is available now."

"Sounds too good to be true."

"It is." He guided her across the pool deck and down a long windy path until her feet finally hit the warm white sand.

The salty air hit her nostrils.

God, she loved that smell. It had been fifteen years since she'd seen the ocean. Of course, the Pacific and the Atlantic were different. California and Florida were two very different states.

But no matter where in the world, when the water hit the sand, it was magical.

"What's wrong with the place?" she asked.

"For starters, it's tiny. One room that houses the kitchen, family room, and bedroom. What's nice about the space is the bed is Murphy style and it pulls out from the wall above a small desk, so it doesn't intrude on the living space. It's got a decent-size bathroom, but only has a shower. No tub."

"I'm not much of a soaker, so that wouldn't matter."

"What's to love is that you'd have access to the pool and it's on the Intracoastal Waterway." He nudged her toward a set of beach chairs. "The view is spectacular."

She eased into one, stretching out her legs, and took a long slow draw of her beer. "Right now, it sounds perfect. How do you know about this place?"

"I'm the owner."

"Now you really sound like a creepy stalker serial killer."

"You sound like someone who reads or watches too many mysteries, but I can assure, I'm none of those things. I just finished renovating the space and was considering listing it for rent. So, the only thing I'm guilty of is impeccable timing."

"Considering?"

"I'm a cop and the son of the chief of police. I can't have just anyone living in my backyard. I'm not sure I would have gone through a regular listing to find a tenant." He sipped his beverage, his gaze locked with hers intently.

It was unnerving how at ease she felt. How comfortable he made her feel in his presence. That should alarm her. In the last fifteen years, she had few relationships with men. In part because she never stayed in one place long enough to have any lasting commitments.

But mostly she didn't trust anyone.

Men or women.

And that included cops.

The system hadn't been kind to her as a kid.

Not to mention if anyone had ever found out what she had done, well, that would land her in cuffs.

This was a bad idea.

"How much?" She'd driven into Lighthouse Cove two weeks ago, stopping at a small motel for the night on her way to Miami. At least that had been the plan. But she'd fallen in love with the quaint seaside town. She'd decided if she found a decent job, she'd stay for a bit.

Safe Harbor Café hired her the next day. They were able to give her plenty of hours and the gift shop around the corner filled in the rest. It wasn't a ton of money, but she didn't need a lot. Just enough to survive.

All she had to do was get out of that god-awful motel. It was run-down and drugs were definitely being sold on a daily basis. She wouldn't be surprised if rooms were sold by the hour. It had been cheap and only fifteen minutes from the center of town. Luckily, she found an ad for a cheapish one-bedroom in a four-unit house. Only the fucking thing was right across the street from the criminally loaded motel.

"That can be negotiated."

She cocked her head. "You have to have a price you're looking for and honestly, I get the feeling I can't afford it because I've been searching and everything on the water is way out of my league."

He set his bottle in the sand, making sure it wouldn't fall over. He shifted his body. "I'm not looking to bleed anyone dry. I don't need the money. If I were to rent it, I'd want—and need—the tenant to be willing to live with a few restrictions because we'd be sharing a few spaces. Namely my pool, something I use a lot. You could have a guest or two, of course, but honestly, I wouldn't want you to have any parties. I'd need to know about anyone spending the night." He arched a brow. "Do you have a boyfriend I need to be aware of?"

She laughed. "That's a personal question, but no. And I doubt I'd ever be having any overnight guests. Or parties. I'm not fond of large gatherings."

"Me either." He smiled.

"I work two jobs. One at Safe Harbor Café and

the other at the Seaside Trinket Shop. That adds up to about sixty hours. I wouldn't be home a lot. When I am home, I like my quiet space, so you wouldn't hear me much." Jesus, what the hell was she doing? Sure, she'd heard about the Kirby family from Lucy Ann and Phil. How they were good people and staples in the community.

But he was a fucking cop.

He and his damned sexy eyes could put her away for a very long time.

"Are you working tomorrow?" he asked.

She nodded. "Breakfast and lunch at the diner."

"Why don't I swing by after your shift and we can go check out the pool house. If you're interested, all I'll need to do is have you fill out an application and I'll let you tell me what you can afford. If I think it's fair, we can go from there." He lifted his beer. "Do you have references from previous places you rented?"

"I do."

"Good." He tipped his longneck and leaned back. "So, I have to ask, what brought you to Lighthouse Cove?"

She had no idea how to answer that question. Every time she moved, someone asked why she chose her next location, and it always tripped her up. She had no family. No clue if her biological parents were dead or alive. There was no rhyme or reason for where she landed. She wandered from place to place because staying anywhere too long meant someone could find her and that wasn't an option.

But she couldn't say that to anyone.

Especially a cop.

Fuck. He'd probably do a background check. Many people did and they always learned a couple of things. None of which made her look good.

Time to turn on that cute charm some told her she had and do some fancy chatting. "I've always been a bit of a nomad and I love exploring new places. I learn so much about history and people that way. It's an adventure and I love finding little hidden gems like this."

"That's intriguing. Mind if I ask why?"

"It's not all that interesting." She took another hearty swig of her beverage, letting the bubbles float in her mouth, enjoying the taste before swallowing. She preferred whiskey or tequila, but this was nice. And the ocean made it even better, taming her emotions.

She did her best to ignore the pull toward the sexy man sitting next to her. She'd met her fair share of guys who got her hot and bothered. She'd had a few fantastic love affairs along the way. Okay, she'd never actually been in love before, but she'd had great sex with some really spicy men. Some had been intellectual. Others creative. A few had been funny. One or two just sexy, badass, gorgeous, and as long as they didn't open their mouth, it was all good. But none of them held her attention long enough to make her want to stay in one place.

Or maybe she was too afraid.

Didn't matter.

Lighthouse Cove, no matter how much she'd already become attached to it more than any other place, was not home.

That would never happen for Rumor Crimson.

Ever.

"It is to a man who has lived in the same town his whole life," he said. "When I was young, I thought about leaving. But it was a fleeting idea. A concept. Once I slapped on the badge, that was it. I was never leaving and honestly, I can't imagine living anywhere else." He waggled a finger. "I have traveled some. My brothers and I have gone out west to go snow skiing and we've been up to Maryland and New York going to different spots. I've even been to London once."

"I've lived all over the country," she admitted. "Seen and been most places that you wouldn't even think of going. I mean, is Lighthouse Cove really a big tourist destination? Or is it one of those sweet little places people stumble upon?"

He chuckled. "We do rely on tourism as part of our economy, but we don't have the draw that places like Miami have." He lowered his chin. "Nor do we want it."

"I still want to make my way down there. Check out the scene." She shrugged. "I generally don't like to land in big cities for very long. I'm a quiet person. I enjoy simple things. Wide-open spaces. Walks on the beach. I don't like crowds."

"Then you won't like Miami at all."

"Probably not, but I also want to see what Key West is like and Miami is on the way."

"Now Key West can be fun. The drive, not so much." Emmerson nodded. "What about your family? Where are they?"

"That's why I move around a lot." She took a big gulp. If she didn't give him a baseline of truth, she'd always be looked at as a woman with secrets. A woman everyone in town should approach with caution. That was not what she wanted or needed. Although, she didn't want to be approached at all. "You see, my parents abandoned me when I was eleven and I went from one foster home to the next until I was eighteen."

Gently, he rested his hand on her wrist. "I'm sorry," he whispered. "That had to have been hard."

"It was," she admitted, staring at his long, strong fingers. Her breath stuck in her throat in a couple of seconds. Men touching her generally didn't have an instant effect. She had to work her way up to attraction. To heat. Desire.

But not with this one.

Her attraction for him was bold. Intoxicating. And palpable.

"Once I became an adult, I felt lost. Nothing

made sense and the last thing I wanted was to be close to anyone I knew in the system. So, I packed up my things and started driving. I've been going from one little town to the next."

"How long have you been doing that?"

"Fifteen years." She lifted her gaze. "I know it sounds weird, but it's honestly been a lot of fun. I've met some interesting people along the way and I've been able to see the country. It's been a trip."

"I imagine it has, but don't you want to find a place to call home?" He released his intimate touch, but not his intent stare.

It was unsettling. But only because she'd enjoyed the way he looked at her, as if he were hanging on her every word.

"I'm sure for you, home is where your family is." She waved her hand over her head toward the massive house and turned her gaze toward the ocean. She needed to be careful how much she gave away. "You have brothers, parents, nieces, and nephews. People to stay connected to. I didn't have good experiences with any of my foster families and while I've enjoyed many of the places this wild journey has taken me on, I always find myself wanting to see more. Experience more. It's almost like I'm looking for my Mount Everest and I simply haven't found it yet." And she needed to keep time and distance from her past.

"I have a buddy who has spent his entire adult life

in the military. Special Forces. He lives for that shit. The idea that someday he's going to have to retire makes him twitch. He's been all over the globe, and he's seen some things. He wouldn't trade that for my sleepy little town and cushy boring police job."

"Everyone has their own path in life and as long as you're living *your* dream, I'm not one to judge."

"Me neither." He stood, holding out his hand. "I better get you back before people start talking."

She lowered her chin.

He chuckled. "You'll learn that in Lighthouse Cove, people gossip. A lot. And one of their favorite pastimes is my family. We're an eclectic bunch with an interesting history."

"I'm not sure if that scares me or fascinates me."

"It should do a little of both." He took her hand, lacing his fingers through hers as if it were the normal thing to do. "I'm happy to give you a little history lesson about my family and Lighthouse Cove tomorrow."

She strolled across the beach with the odd sensation building in the pit of her stomach. Most men she could take or leave.

Something told her that Emmerson wasn't most men.

She doubted he was dangerous, at least not in terms of causing her bodily harm. Over the years, thanks in part to her experience with Tony and a few other mistakes with trusting people she shouldn't, she'd developed a sense about people, and Emmerson projected all that was good in this world.

As did the rest of the men in his family.

Hell, everyone she'd met at this party had given her a good vibe.

But she still needed to be apprehensive.

That didn't mean she couldn't lease his pool house.

"I have one more question about your rental," she said as they approached the walkway back to the main house.

"What's that?"

"Is it fully furnished? I have nothing and that would be helpful."

He laughed. "If you call a bed, a desk, a table, a couch, and a big-screen TV furnished, then yes, it is," he said. "Oh, and it does have pots, pans, plates, and all that. Whatever it doesn't have that you need, I'll be happy to provide."

"I don't need much, so I'm sure I'll be fine." She tugged her hand away. The last thing she needed was anyone seeing that. She wasn't sure why she allowed it to last as long as she had. Giving him the wrong impression wouldn't be a good idea if she were to rent his pool house.

He pressed his hand on the small of her back and guided her back onto the pool deck. "Looks like some of my family has left."

"I'm sorry you didn't get a chance to say goodbye."

He shrugged. "I see them almost every day. It's not the end of the world."

"I should get going." She tugged her shirt closed, fastening the buttons. "Thanks for showing me the beach. It was lovely. I'll see you tomorrow after the lunch shift. I get off around four."

"Let's exchange numbers. I'll still be on duty, so it's possible something could happen that could cause me to be late. If that's the case, we can meet at my place, but I wouldn't want you to think I was standing you up." He pulled his cell from his shorts. "Why don't you put in your number and text yourself?"

She did as he requested. "We can meet later, if you'd like."

"It's fine. I'm working an overnight for my brother. Whenever any of us works a double like that, my mother forces us to take a couple of hours rest. Technically, it's not until a little later, so I'll need to leave my radio on in case a call comes over. But I can spare a couple of hours to show you the place and I've got to eat dinner anyway."

"All right." She handed over his phone. "I better be on my way." She snagged her bag from behind the bar. "It was nice seeing you again and I look forward to checking out the pool house."

"Drive safe." He squeezed her biceps.

She nodded, turned on her heel, and made a beeline for the side entrance.

Hopefully, he'd be good with a three-month lease, because that's all she intended to give this town. Save up a little money, have a few adventures, and then she'd be on her way south. If she didn't like Miami, she'd check out the Keys.

Then make her way north through the Carolinas, Virginia, Maryland, Vermont, Maine, maybe even New York.

There was still so much to see and experience.

She paused at her new vehicle—well, new to her—and glanced over her shoulder. The big house on the ocean stood tall and proud. In all her years, she'd never been inside anything so beautiful. Not even when she cleaned houses in a posh neighborhood outside of Knoxville, Tennessee. She sighed, dumping her bag into the passenger seat.

Lighthouse Cove certainly had been an unexpected stop that filled her gut with butterflies.

Something she hadn't experienced in years.

Emmerson snagged a beer and strolled across the pool deck toward Jameson and Miles, who sat at the shallow end of the pool with their feet dangling in the water.

Jameson was the baby of the family, but he'd

managed to pump out two little ones already. His oldest, he adopted shortly after she'd been born. His two younger ones came right after.

Miles was still single and he liked it that way. He was forty and had not a single prospect for a girlfriend in sight.

Neither did Emmerson.

Well, he was hoping Rumor had increased those odds.

"How's it going?" Emmerson joined his brothers, easing his feet into the warm water.

"We should be asking you that." Jameson laughed. "Did you get yourself a date?"

"I wouldn't call it that." Emmerson took a long slow draw from his beer.

"Rhett told me you're thinking about renting her the pool house," Miles said. "He's already looking into her background."

Emmerson cringed. "Is nothing sacred in this family?" He rubbed the back of his neck. "You better not tell Mom he's poking around."

"Do you think we're stupid?" Jameson laughed. "But why the contorted look? Did he find something already?"

Emmerson shook his head. "I learned something the old-fashioned way, but Rhett will see it as a red flag. I view it as a girl who had a shitty childhood and is simply trying to find her place in this world."

"Wow. You got all that from a walk on the beach?" Jameson glanced at his watch. "In an hour's time?"

"I'm a cop. I know how to ask the right questions." The last thing Emmerson wanted to do was gossip about the new girl with his little brothers, even if they were good sounding boards.

"Dating your tenant could get awkward," Jameson said.

"No one said anything about me taking her out." Emmerson wanted nothing more than to get to know Rumor better, and that included romantically. However, his cop instincts had been set into high alert during their conversation.

And not because of what she'd told him about her past.

It was because of what she hadn't told him and the way she averted her gaze during part of their talk. She gave just enough detail to make a normal person feel satisfied about her answers, but for him, he needed more.

No one spent fifteen years going from one place to the next, living on pennies, unless they were running from something.

Or hiding.

He almost wished he could tell Rhett to back off. Rhett was the best private investigator Emmerson knew. If there was something to learn, Rhett would uncover it.

Part of Emmerson wanted to figure it out on his

own. Peel back the layers one mystery at a time. However, that wouldn't be smart. Not if she was going to live in his backyard.

"Oh, come on, man," Miles said. "We all have been watching you drool over her all day."

"That's a stretch." Emmerson set his beer down and leaned back on his hands. "I'll admit, she's pretty and all that, but she's too young for this old man."

"I call bullshit on that," Jameson said. "Age is just a number and she's what, maybe ten years younger? Why won't you go for it?"

"Do you really want the laundry list?" Emmerson asked.

"We do. That way we can start crossing off your stupid reasons why and get you motivated to actually have a love life again." Miles raised his drink. "Lord knows you need one. You're ornery as fuck lately."

"You're one to talk." Emmerson laughed. "When was the last time you went out with anyone?"

"Last week." Miles cocked a brow. "I'm at least getting action."

Jameson burst out laughing. "You're going through ladies so fast lately that no one will have anything to do with you in this town. How are you ever going to find a good woman to settle down with?"

"Who says I want to settle down?" Miles asked. "Not everyone wants a white picket fence, a couple of kids, and a dog. Besides, we're not talking about me; we're talking about Emmerson."

"I'm doing just fine on my own, thank you very much." The only problem with that statement was that Emmerson had wanted what all his married brothers had. At least he had thought he did. Now? He wondered if that ship had sailed. He was set in his ways and he wasn't sure he wanted to change for any woman.

He loved his career. His family meant the world to him, and his life was comfortable.

"Hey, Emmerson." His mother appeared at his side. "Are you sober?"

"I am. Why?"

"How sober?" His mother pointed to the beer by his side and glared. "I need to know how much you've had to drink."

"That's my third beer in the last three hours and I've barely touched it," Emmerson said.

"Where's your uniform?" his mother asked.

"In my vehicle. Why? What's going on?" Emmerson jumped to his feet. He knew his mother well and when she got like this, something big had happened.

"Emmett is in no shape and Nathan has to deal with the kids. I need a seasoned detective over at the Seaside Motel to help Chris Manzo. There's been a murder."

"Jesus," Emmerson muttered. "Any other details?"

"All I know is that the front desk got an anonymous call that two women were screaming at each other in a room. When management went to check on it, they accessed the room to find a woman lying on the floor in a pool of blood after being stabbed to death. No suspects as of right now. Chris is doing what he can, but he's a rookie."

"All right. I'll go change and head over now," Emmerson said.

"Thanks. Keep me informed. I'll be out there as soon as I can." His mom squeezed his biceps. "Be safe out there, son."

He leaned in and kissed his mother's cheek. "I always am."

Not much happened in Lighthouse Cove, but when it did, it happened big.

3

Rumor glanced out the window. It had been a while since the man and woman had been fighting in the parking lot. She'd tried not to look at them as she scurried from her car to the front door. After all these years, she knew better than to insert herself into other people's business.

She let out a sigh and leaned back, lifting her book. She needed to get the fuck out of this part of town. The one thing she was tired of was living in hellholes.

And she needed to be careful with her suitcase full of cash. She knew it was stupid. And some of that money she'd earned.

But the majority of it was stolen.

From a drug dealer.

Knock. Knock.

Rumor jerked at the sound. She checked the time.

It was only eight, so not late, but who the hell would be paying her a visit?

She jumped off the sofa and raced to the door, looking through the peephole.

A fucking cop?

What the hell?

Her heart hammered in her chest. For the last fifteen years, she'd managed to stay clear of all law enforcement. She'd never gotten a ticket of any kind. She'd kept herself out of trouble at all costs.

Tentatively, she opened the door. "Um, hello," she said, noticing two police cars, a fire truck, the medical examiner's vehicle, and an ambulance in front of the motel across the street.

She had to get out of this neighborhood.

"Sorry to bother you, ma'am. I'm Deputy Chris Manzo with the Lighthouse Cove Police Department. I'm checking with all the neighbors in the area to find out if they heard or saw anything disturbing across the street in the last couple of hours."

The last thing Rumor wanted to do was get involved in a police investigation of any kind. But she didn't want to lie either. That would get her in hot water in a different way.

"I wouldn't say it was disturbing, but I did see a woman and a man fighting in the parking lot when I came home. I didn't pay too much attention to it because it didn't look troubling."

"Can you give me a description of the woman?"

"She had long dark hair, pulled back into a ponytail. She was wearing shorts and T-shirt. But that's all I remember about her," Rumor said, gripping the door.

The deputy glanced over his shoulder. "Could you please come with me and give a statement of what you saw with our detective?"

Shit. God, she wanted to say no. Being a witness to anything would be a bad idea. But what could she do? "Sure. Can I go get my shoes?"

"Why don't you wait right here and I'll send Detective Kirby over."

Fucking wonderful. One of the Kirby brothers. Just what she needed.

"Okay," she said.

She watched as Deputy Manzo strolled across the street while she stepped out onto the small porch. She suspected that if Lighthouse Cove had a bad section of town, this would be it.

When she'd booked the short-term rental, she'd found the listing had been shut down on Airbnb and the reviews had made her leery, but she reminded herself that it was temporary, and she'd lived in worse.

The other police officer—the detective—turned.

Her breath flew from her lungs like an eagle taking flight.

Emmerson. With two *M*'s.

Hot. Sexy. Made her loose in the lips.

Emmerson.

At least it was a familiar face. Not that his brothers weren't, but she had a better sense of who Emmerson was and how he might treat her, or at least she hoped.

Emmerson glanced both ways before crossing the street. He waved and gave her a half smile. "Hey." He jogged up the steps. "My deputy tells me you saw a man and a woman arguing in the parking lot?"

She nodded.

"Unfortunately, the description you gave of the woman matches that of the girl who was found murdered in one of the rooms," he said.

She gasped, covering her mouth and stumbling backward.

Tony… murder… dead body… police… the past she'd run from? The past she'd done her best to bury had reached out, grabbed her ankle, and now she was face down on the floorboards.

In a flash, Lighthouse Cove had lost its allure.

Emmerson inched closer. He rested his strong hand on her shoulder. "I'm sorry. I should have been more tactful in how I said that. I don't mean to scare you."

"No. It's okay. I'm just in shock. I mean, I didn't think too much about people having a heated discussion in a parking lot. It happens and it's not my business."

"I know this is difficult, but can you tell me what you saw? What you heard?"

"I didn't really hear anything. Just raised voices."

"All right." Emmerson looped his fingers into his belt and took a cop stance, making her want to run. And run fast. "Did either one seem more aggressive than the other? Were you concerned for your safety? Or either of theirs?"

"I honestly didn't stand around and watch," Rumor said. "I got out of my car and heard a man's voice, so I looked across the street. He was kind of in her face, and she waved her hands frantically. I scurried up the steps, shut my door, and took a shower. I didn't hear or see anything else."

"What did this man look like? What was he wearing?" Emmerson jerked his thumb over his shoulder. "Did you notice any other vehicles in the parking lot other than the ones there now?"

She blew out a puff of air. "Um. He was youngish. Maybe thirty something. Blond hair, cut short. I think he was wearing jeans and a dark shirt, but I can't be sure and I have no idea about the cars."

"Nothing else?"

She shook her head. "Not that I can think of. I'm sorry."

"That's okay. You've been incredibly helpful." He smiled, waving his hand over her pathetic folding chair. "Why don't you take a seat and hang tight for a few minutes. I need to go talk to Chris and handle a few things, and then I'll be back."

"I'm tired. I need to get up early."

"I won't be too long." He squeezed her shoulder before turning and racing off across the street.

Wonderful.

She fell back in the rusted old chair with a grunt. She watched as Emmerson chatted with the other cop before turning his attention to the medical examiner who exited the motel room with the gurney.

She swallowed the thick lump in her throat.

The first and last time she saw a dead body was fifteen years ago. A memory that would forever be etched into her psyche, but she wished she could forget. It haunted her daily existence and visited her in her nightmares.

No matter where in the world she ended up, that damn dead body found her.

God, she wished this chair had been a rocker. She crossed and uncrossed her legs a dozen times while she watched Emmerson do cop-like things.

Whatever they were.

The ambulance pulled out of the parking lot, followed the medical examiner, and finally, the fire truck.

All that remained were the two cops.

Emmerson and Deputy Manzo stood in front of the motel for what seemed like a half hour. But since Rumor timed it, she knew it was only eleven minutes. Emmerson pointed to a few things before Manzo ducked under the crime scene tape and disappeared into one of the rooms.

She stood and leaned against the half-rotted railing. On the outside, she knew she appeared calm, but on the inside, she shook like a volcano on the verge of erupting.

He raked his hand across the top of his head. "I had no idea you were staying on this side of town."

"It was all that was available."

"What about the bed and breakfast in town?"

"Too expensive," she said. "My funds are limited." While she was a proud woman, she had no problem not only being frugal, but admitting that she needed to be. Based on the way his mother lived, she wondered if he could even understand that concept.

"Yeah. I get it. Melinda's rates can be pricey. Especially this time of year." He glanced over his shoulder. "In general, most places in Lighthouse Cove are safe, but this area lately has been nothing but trouble. I can't get into all of it, but my mom is concerned about a drug ring that's been working the East Coast from Miami all the way to Maryland. I'm wondering if this murder has anything to do with it since we did have a bust here a week ago." He let out a long breath. "I don't like you staying here alone."

"I'll be fine. I'm used to taking care of myself." Her first stop in Tennessee had been Memphis. The one thing she'd remembered about her parents had been they were big Elvis fans. They loved music of all kinds, but Elvis was one of their favorites. Visiting Graceland had been one of those things she had to do. The little girl in her hoped she'd run into her parents on the streets of Memphis. The adult knew that was a fantasy. Yet she felt compelled to visit. However, it had to be one of the most dangerous cities she ever set foot in. She stayed in a dumpy motel for three nights. That had been enough. She toured Graceland and moved on to Nashville where she stayed for a couple months and eventually Knoxville.

Now that had been a great place to live.

"Well, I won't sleep well if you're staying here tonight. Not when I have a perfectly good pool house waiting for you to rent in a nice neighborhood," he said. "Besides, I'm sure we can come to an agreement on rent. Why don't you pack a few things and we can get the rest tomorrow."

She folded her arms across her chest. "No offense, but I doubt whoever did this will be coming back."

He tilted his head. "I've been a cop for twenty years and one of the biggest things I've learned is the perp always comes back to the scene of the crime. They can't help themselves." He planted his hands on his hips. "Look. Generally, this is a sleepy little town and murders don't happen every day. It's my job to keep people safe."

"Are you going to ask everyone who lives on this street to come stay at your house?"

"No." He scratched the back of his head. "But you've got another, safer option. In the last two weeks we've had a wave of drugs coming through town that has baffled us and now this. Just take what I'm offering. I'll feel better and you won't have to deal with this run-down rental anymore." He held up his hand. "The owner isn't even supposed to be leasing any rooms in this house. We've shut him down twice and come tomorrow, now that I know he's done it again, you'll be asked to leave anyway."

"What? I answered a flyer hanging in—"

"My point exactly. It wasn't in the app." He arched a brow. "This house has code violations with the town that haven't been fixed. He doesn't have fire escapes or fire alarms. I'm sure he never fixed the back window and there's still cardboard covering it."

She nodded. No point in lying.

"I could go on, listing all the issues, but the owner has been warned numerous times that this house has to be brought up to code before anyone can live in it and he certainly can't rent it."

"So, you're going to strong-arm me into leaving." It wasn't a question, but a statement of fact.

"Yes," he said. "But I'm not doing it because I'm being a dick. I wouldn't have said anything until tomorrow, except you're fighting me on this, so I'm driving the point home."

"No, you're pushing the weight of your badge in my face and I don't appreciate it." She turned on her heel and gripped the door handle. "I'll need fifteen minutes to collect what I need."

"I'll wait."

"Of course you will." She stormed into the house and raced up the stairs. She could pack everything she owned in a matter of minutes. She didn't collect things. All she had was two suitcases that housed her clothes and a backpack for her electronics.

And because this little rental wasn't a place she planned on calling home for any length of time, she had literally been living out of her suitcases, not bothering to unpack.

She quickly snagged the few things she had in the bathroom, tossing them into her bag.

"Hey, do you need a hand?" Emmerson called.

"If you want to pack the few food items I have in the kitchen, feel free."

"I think I can handle that."

As quickly as she could, she finished in the bedroom. She hoisted her backpack over her shoulder and lifted the suitcase with her money and carried it down the steps. "I've got one more bag upstairs."

"Let's put all this stuff in your car, and then I'll go get it." Emmerson stood in the family room holding two bags. "Is there anything else in here that's yours?"

"Nope. But I'm supposed to clean this place, strip the bed, and take out the trash before I leave, or I'll get dinged with a cleaning fee."

"No, you won't," he said. "And I'll make sure you get your rent back. What did you pay for this place?"

"Two fifty for the week." She followed Emmerson out the door.

He mumbled something under his breath.

"This is me." She pulled out her key fob and unlocked her vehicle.

"All right. Stay right here. I'll go get your other bag, and then you can follow me back to my place. We'll hammer out the lease agreement tomorrow after work."

"Um, are you good with a three-month rental?"

"Yeah, sure, that's fine." He nodded. "Hang tight."

He raced off down the sidewalk.

She cocked her head. Damn, he had a sexy swagger, even when he was being a total controlling asshole.

But he was right. That house was a shithole. Nothing worked right. The toaster nearly electrocuted her the first time she tried to use it. There was no hot water and when she complained, the asshole who owned the place told her she probably wasn't turning the knob the right way.

Worse, the water that came out of the faucet was this weird light-brown color. She wasn't about to drink that shit, so she had to buy bottled.

The air conditioning barely worked, so she'd sweat like crazy at night. Half the time she slept on the sofa downstairs. Emmerson offering to let her go to his place should be seen as a godsend.

But it wasn't.

Not anymore.

Now she was a potential witness in a murder investigation.

The same exact fucking thing she'd been running from for fifteen years.

Emmerson checked his rearview mirror. Rumor was right on his tail. He tapped his cell, calling his mother. He put the phone on speaker and set it on the cradle on the dash.

This conversation wasn't going to go well.

"Hey, Emmerson. Is the CSI unit there?" his mother asked. "I'll be heading out there in twenty."

"They weren't there when I left," he said. "I was told they would be there shortly. Chris is managing things."

"Why did you leave?"

"That's an interesting story." He stopped at the red light in the center of town and flipped on his blinker, heading toward the bridge.

"I'm all ears."

"Rumor, the girl you hired to work the party, the one you were all hot to fix me up with, well, she was renting the Crawly house."

"Fuck. That man is going to end up in jail now. How many times is he going to pull this shit? That house is seconds from being condemned," his mom said. "But what does that have to do with this murder?"

"She witnessed an argument in the parking lot with the victim and a man. But whoever called this in, specifically said the victim was in a screaming match with a woman. There is a slight time difference in this when I put it all together."

"What do you mean?"

"Rumor came home from your party and saw a man with the victim approximately thirty minutes before the anonymous call came in. Our victim could have had two different fights."

"That's certainly possible," his mother said. "Did she get a good look at this man?"

"Not really, but tomorrow I'll get a sketch artist to come out and talk with Rumor. I've already put a call into the county for that."

"Okay. Good. But that still doesn't explain why you left a rookie at the scene to deal with CSI."

He punched the gas when the arrow turned green. Thankfully, the bridge was down. He drove over the Intracoastal Waterway and made a right turn. His neighborhood was only five minutes away. It was right near the inlet and he had a great view of the boats coming and going to the ocean. "Well, I couldn't let her stay at Crawly's. I'll deal with him as well tomorrow. But for now, Rumor will be renting my pool house."

"Jesus, Emmerson. She's a fucking witness now. Are you crazy?"

"I had already offered it to her anyway."

"So? You could have found something else for her, especially considering she's now involved in this case."

Emmerson rolled his eyes. "She saw two people having a disagreement. I'll get her settled, and then I'm headed back to the motel. I'll see you there shortly."

"You haven't even done a proper background check on this girl."

He laughed. "Ma, I love you. I'm on it and I'll talk to you soon." He tapped the red button and pulled into his driveway, opening the garage. He stepped from the vehicle. "You can park under the carport." He motioned to the side of the garage.

Rumor nodded and eased her car around the side of the house, popping her trunk.

He pulled out the two suitcases. "Follow me."

"I'm not sure what I expected, but this is beautiful. How long have you lived here?"

"Two years," Emmerson said as he strolled around the side of the house. As soon as he passed the main bushes, the lights flicked on. He pushed open the gate to the pool. "All my brothers were either married with kids or getting married and buying places on the water. I guess I got a little jealous and decided to join them. Jameson lives five houses down the street. Nathan and Seth across the water. Rhett lives up the river. By boat it's about thirty minutes. By car, maybe ten minutes. Emmett and his wife live up the Intracoastal about ten minutes away. Miles is the only one not living on the water. But he's got the bug." He dug into his pocket and pulled out the pool house keys. "I'm sorry I can't show you around, but I do have to get back to the motel."

"I'll be fine."

He pushed open the door. "When I bought this place, the pool house was nothing but a storage room. I finished renovating it a couple of weeks ago." He turned on the main light. "It's not much, but like I said, you can use the pool anytime you want. Tomorrow, I'll help you download the app for the hot tub. I also have a couple of kayaks and paddleboards. Feel free to use those as well."

"Seriously?"

"There are four of them, and I only need one. However, sometimes Miles comes over and we go out together. And I will warn you that occasionally my brothers and their kids come over."

"It's your house."

He pushed the suitcases to the side. "The television is loaded with all the streaming services." He pointed to the remote on the coffee table in front of the small white leather sofa that his mom had given him when she'd replaced her sitting room furniture.

"The stove is brand new. So is the fridge and microwave."

"This place is amazing," she said softly, running her fingers over the side of the couch. "I honestly don't think I can afford it."

"Don't worry about that." He closed the gap between them but resisted the urge to wrap his arms around Rumor and pull her close. Trust didn't come easily to Emmerson. Not when it came to women, and Rumor had secrets. He could see that when he looked deep into her eyes. He believed everything she had told him about what she'd seen earlier tonight. He had no doubt about that.

But it triggered something that had caused her to recoil. He sensed a distance that wasn't there before. While she'd been reserved at his mother's house, only giving him surface level information, he could understand why. They were just getting to know one another and she was a wanderer. A person who didn't make lasting connections.

He could relate to that.

The only deep connections he had with anyone were with his family and a few close friends whom he'd known since childhood.

Thanks to Edwina and fucking Tessa, opening his heart to a woman had become impossible.

And yet he wanted Rumor like he hadn't wanted another woman in years.

However, there was a black shadow that clung to her like thick fog on a stormy night, daring the ships to try to pass.

She was hiding something and he was desperate to know that secret and why she was so compelled to keep it tucked away in a vault.

"I have to be concerned about that because you could get four grand a month for this place just because it's on the water. I could only swing a grand. That math doesn't add up."

"I'll accept a thousand dollars a month." He smiled.

"That's ridiculous."

"Not for me. Not when it's a three-month lease and I'm doing it as a trial run to see if I even want to continue renting the place. Hell, we can go month to month or even week to week. If you don't like it here, you can move."

"Why are you helping me?" she asked, holding his gaze with questioning and untrusting eyes.

He had to ask himself, would he trust the situation? Would he look at himself the same way?

What were his motivations?

He couldn't honestly answer those questions without looking like an asshole.

The reality was, he wanted her close. He didn't know why. It was about the craziest thing he'd ever done, outside of moving in with Tessa.

That had been one hell of a mistake.

But Rumor wasn't Tessa. Rumor was a girl with a shitty past.

Fuck, and a chick with a secret.

He sure knew how to pick them.

"Because I want to and because I can," he said. "Let me show you how this bed works, and then I really have to go." He turned and reached for the Murphy bed over the desk. "It's really simple. All you have to do is pull on the handle and it folds down. The sheets are clean and the pillows are in the drawers in the coffee table."

"That's convenient."

"Here are the keys." He dangled them in his hands. "Call or text if you need anything or have any questions. I have no idea if I'll be back before you have to leave for work. If I don't see you before that, I'll stop by at the diner," he said. "Oh, and I do need you to make an official statement and talk to a sketch artist. We'll set that up tomorrow."

"Ugh. Do I have to?"

"Unfortunately, yes. Whoever that man was that you saw, we have no idea who he is or where he is. If he killed that girl, he's still out there, and he's danger-ous. Lock the doors behind me. I have security cameras outside. I'll be alerted if there is movement."

"So, you'll see me coming and going?"

"I'm not going to spy on you." He arched a brow. "And there are no cameras inside here, so you don't have to worry about that." He curled his fingers around her biceps. "You'll be safe here." He leaned in and kissed her cheek.

She didn't jerk away.

But she did tense up.

Damn.

4

———————

Rumor took her mug of coffee and stepped out onto the pool deck. The sun had yet to appear. It wasn't even five in the morning yet and she had to be to work by six. The nice thing about living this close to town was she could walk to work if she wanted to and since she'd gotten up so early, that's exactly what she planned on doing.

Right after she enjoyed a cup of Joe on the dock while watching a few of the boats cruising by as they headed out into the ocean.

God, this was the life.

One she didn't dare get used to.

She'd slept like a fucking baby in that damn Murphy bed. It was the most comfortable mattress she'd ever slept on. The temperature of the room had been perfect. She felt like fucking Goldilocks. Everything was just right.

Safe didn't begin to describe the sensation she'd felt when she'd closed her eyes.

She had no reason to fear Emmerson. Only his badge.

Which made this entire situation insane.

As she made her way toward the dock on a path lit up by cute little lights that were just bright enough to make it easy on her eyes, she thought about all the places she'd lived before.

The first few had been god-awful. She'd been so afraid to pull out any of those bills, but she was even more terrified to use her credit card. Those first few months she moved what seemed like every month, taking whatever nasty cleaning job she could find along the way.

Almost all the rentals she'd ever called home the first five years were in neighborhoods much like where the murder had occurred last night. She always tried to find safe places, but when you lived paycheck to paycheck and your skill set was limited, finding decent housing when you wanted to live alone became difficult.

But as she scrimped and saved and put some of her own money away, making it easier to stop dipping into the bag of cash, and actually adding to it, she found better places to live. Though sometimes that took some looking and effort on her part.

The moment her foot hit the dock, she paused, staring at a massive center console boat with twin engines. It was big and shiny and beautiful. The name of the boat was *Just the Facts*.

She chuckled.

"What's so funny?" a male voice echoed from somewhere to her right.

"Who's there?" She squinted, glancing toward a set of chairs on the dock overlooking the waterway.

"Just Emmerson." He waved his hand. "Good morning. Did you sleep well?"

"I did. Thank you, but you scared the shit out of me."

"I'm sorry. I'm often down here in the morning. Sunrises are the best right here." He patted the chair next to him. "Join me if you have time."

As she inched closer, she realized he was in his uniform. "Heading back out to work soon?"

"I just got home about a half hour ago." He raised a mug and sipped. "I came home for some food, a shower, and then I have to go to the station. It's going to be a long day for me."

She lowered herself into the Adirondack chair and stared at Emmerson's strong profile. A five o'clock shadow had appeared on his face, making him look even more handsome, if that were possible. There was a genuine kindness about him that she couldn't deny. "Did you catch the person who killed that girl?"

"Sadly, no. And we have very few leads." He turned his head. "One of the things on my long list today was to come talk to you again."

"To give my official statement?"

"Yes and no. My mother would like you to do that with one of my brothers at the station when you get off work. The sketch artist will be there too so you can give details about the man you saw."

"I didn't get that great of a look, so I'm not sure I'll be of any real help there."

He shifted. "Are you sure it was a man you saw?"

"The voice was deep and he looked like a man to me. Why do you ask?"

Emmerson let out a long breath. "We got an anonymous tip that the victim was arguing with a woman. That's what I was going to come talk to you about. To get clarification."

She swallowed. Hard. "I'm sorry, Emmerson, but I'm pretty sure it was a man. I suppose I could be wrong; I just don't think I am."

"There's nothing to be sorry about. The victim could have argued with two different people based on the timeline. It just makes my job that much harder when you're the only person who saw her with a man." He reached out and placed his hand over hers and squeezed. "Is there anything else you can remember about last night that might be helpful? Any words spoken by the victim or this man? Money exchanged. Drugs. A physical altercation. Anything."

She stared into his intense dark eyes. She could tell this case tormented his heart and that tore at his soul. She reached into her mind, recalling the moments she pulled up next to the rental and stepped from her car. The man and the woman were standing in the parking lot. The woman waved her hands aggressively. They shouted at one another.

But for the life of her, she couldn't recall a single word.

She'd scurried up the steps and into the house, not wanting to be part of anyone else's problems. For fifteen years she managed to stay clear of trouble. She never engaged in heated discussions. She never argued with anyone. The moment anything got wonky, she hit the road.

"I wasn't outside for any longer than it took me to go from my car to the house and I honestly ignored the two people fighting. It wasn't my business, and unless he was hurting her, I was staying out of it." And if that had been the case, she would have called the police anonymously and hauled ass to Miami.

"If I were you, I probably would have done the same thing in that situation." He ran his thumb over the top of her hand in a tender circle. It felt intimate. Personal.

She should pull away, but instead, she enjoyed the moment.

In the last fifteen years, there had only been a couple of men she'd grown to care for more than she should. One in particular, George, had made it difficult for her to pack up and leave. He had tugged at her heart, filling it with promises of a life she couldn't have. A life that lived in novels and movies. She would admire it from a distance, live vicariously through characters, but never experience it herself.

She left without saying goodbye and she never allowed herself to get that emotionally close to a man again.

That had been eight years ago.

She'd matured since then and had learned how to gauge her emotions better. However, Emmerson and his damn sexy personality came in like a hurricane, tossing her about like a shipwreck. And then, as soon as the seas calmed, he lulled her into his harbor, promising her protection from the storm.

"I wish I could be more help," she whispered. And that was the truth. She could feel the desperation seeping from his pores. The anguish glowed from his dark eyes like the light from the lighthouse stretching across the sky in search of ships to guide home.

He lifted her hand and kissed the inside of her palm, letting his lips linger on her skin.

It took her breath away and ignited a fire in the pit of her stomach. There have been plenty of men where attraction swirled around her insides like a tidal wave. But she had no problem controlling it. With Emmerson, there was no squelching it, and she tried.

"You've been incredibly helpful. It was a rough night. We're a quiet community. I'm a small-town cop who deals with petty crimes, hands out speeding tickets, and tries to keep Old Lady Gardner from killing someone with her garden hose."

"Her hose? This I have to hear." She found herself hanging on his every word, not only intrigued by the tale, but interested in the man. It baffled her mind.

And her heart.

Rumor didn't fall for guys in an instant. She could take them or leave them, having short-lived affairs with men who offered good conversation and sexual release. Emmerson certainly fell into that category. However, he tickled so much more and that scared and excited her in ways she had never experienced.

Emmerson let out a short laugh. "She gets pissed off when people speed down her street, and rightfully so. Instead of calling the police, she takes matters into her own hands by hosing every car down as they drive by. Last time she did it with a pressure washer. She broke two windows and Petey McGuire ended up crashing into a tree." He shook his head. "What was worse, I had to take her to the hospital because it was turned on full blast. Too much for her to handle and she fell on her ass, breaking her tailbone." He ran a hand over his mouth, covering a slight smile.

"You're not laughing, are you?"

"I'm seriously trying not to. Petey wanted me to press charges, and honestly, it was a chargeable offense. But she's sixty-four years old and generally a nice lady. He's not a bad guy, just grumpy since his wife died five years ago, and I have clocked him going through that neighborhood at fifteen over the speed limit. I swear to God, those two have pent-up sexual tension for each other and need to—"

"Are you suggesting they both need to get laid?"

"Your words. Not mine." He lowered his chin. "But thanks to a little meddling on my part, I did hear they went on a date last week." He waggled his brow. "Hopefully that puts an end to those calls."

She turned, tugging the chair closer. "I can't imagine what your job must be like. You're the first cop I've ever spent any time with and I have to say I'm fascinated." She shouldn't be. She should be keeping a safe distance. Being friendly was one thing, but engaging him on a more personal level was a recipe for disaster.

"Most days it's kind of boring. Every once in a while something big happens. Like when Trinity's biological father got himself shot when he'd been wrongfully accused of a string of murders south of here."

"Oh. Oh." She grabbed his arm. "I heard about that from Lucy Ann. Didn't he get shot by federal offi-cers right outside of Safe Harbor Café?"

Emmerson nodded, releasing her hand. "It wasn't our case. Most big ones like that aren't. We just don't have the resources. Either we work with the sheriff or it goes to State. With what happened to Trinity's father, that went through the Feds, but it was a whole shit show. And then there was what went down with Rhett's wife and her brother. You met him." He lifted his mug and sipped.

"I did." She rested her chin in the palm of her hand. She could listen to Emmerson talk all day. The tone of his voice had a calming effect. His eyes were warm and welcoming. Everything about him screamed kindness.

"Yeah. My deputy, Chris Manzo. That's Rhett's brother-in-law. Good man, but he and his wife got mixed up in some crazy mob shit up in New Jersey. Once again, not our case, but we helped. It's kind of what we do."

"Sounds like you really enjoy your job." She smiled. "Helping people, that is."

"Everyone in my family is a bit of bleeding heart that way." He chuckled. "My dad and my brother Seth often do lawyer shit for free. Of course, there are all the cops in the family. We have the firefighter and two private dicks, although one of them is a full-time mechanic who often gives out free oil changes to people who can't pay, which is no way to run a business."

"I'll have to remember that, since I'm due for that and a tire rotation."

"I'll make sure Miles gives you the friends and family deal."

She glanced at her watch. "Oh, shit. I've got to get going. I can't be late for work."

"I'll walk you to your car."

"Emmerson, you don't have to do that. You're dead-dog-tired and need to go to the station. Sit. Relax. Close your eyes."

"If I do that, I'll be asleep in seconds." He pushed from the chair.

"I need to get my bag."

"I'll wait."

"Of course you will." She scurried off into the pool house with her heart in her throat. Everything about Emmerson had thrown her off-kilter. He was everything she fantasized a man should be, and in the same breath, he was everything she avoided. There had been times she thought enough time had passed. But Tony was a grudge holder. He'd never forget she'd been the one to betray him.

Grabbing her purse, she raced back out the door, tugging it to make sure it locked. She'd hidden the bag of money, but that didn't mean it couldn't be found. "Okay. Ready."

"I can come by and bring you to the station for your statement after your shift, if you'd like." He pressed his hand on the small of her back, guiding her across the pool deck.

The closer she got to her vehicle, the closer his hand got to her hip. It wasn't a blatant sexual move, but he wasn't simply being a gentleman either. Especially when he turned her, resting both hands on her waist.

Her arms clung at her sides awkwardly. She was used to being in control of all her dating situations. She decided who and when and this should be no different. The problem was she couldn't deny she wanted Emmerson. But she also struggled to separate the sex from the emotion. Something that hadn't happened since George and she swore she'd never let it happen again.

"I wouldn't want to put you out."

"You're not," he said. "I wish I was the one taking it, but my mother thinks it's best if someone else does it."

She narrowed her stare. "Why?"

"You're an interesting complication." He tilted her chin with his thumb and forefinger. "Tell me this isn't a good idea. Or that you're not interested. Or even if you are, give me a reason I shouldn't kiss you. Otherwise, in about five seconds or less, I'm going for it."

She stared into his liquid gold eyes while she searched for the words. Any words.

But none came.

Next thing she knew, she parted her lips and blinked her eyes closed as his sweet lips landed on hers in one of the most electrifying kisses she'd ever tasted. It was one of those first kisses that you knew you would always remember every single second of. The way his mouth molded perfectly against hers, as if she were the shore and he were the ocean.

The way his tongue eased between her lips,

swirling around hers in a new, but almost familiar dance.

She didn't want the kiss to end, but for her sanity, she needed it to. Fisting his shirt, she took a step back, breaking off what would go down as the kiss to end all kisses. "I really need to go. I was going to walk to work, but now I'm going to have to—"

"I'll drive you." He laced his fingers between hers and tugged.

"No. That's not necessary. Seriously, you need to rest and I get the feeling you're the kind of man who puts everyone else's needs above your own."

"It's the nature of my job." He chuckled. "But it will be easier if I drive you. That way we won't have two cars when I pick you up for your statement."

She stopped dead in her tracks, staring at his police car. "You expect me to get in that thing?"

"My personal car is at the station. I have a motorcycle, but it's at Miles' shop. I pick it up next week."

"Do I have to get in the back? Because that would be way too weird for me and I'd prefer to drive myself if that's the case."

He burst out laughing.

"I don't see why that's got you cracking up."

He cleared his throat, pulling out a key fob. He yanked open the front passenger side door. "The back seat is reserved for those I put in handcuffs." He waved his hand. "I don't intend on using those on you."

"I guess you're not into kinky stuff." She groaned. Over the years she'd learned to keep the flirting to a minimum. Men liked it too much and it always gave the wrong impression. She could get her point across when she was attracted to someone with a lot less fanfare. Keeping men at a safe distance—even those she had short flings with—was a necessary evil.

He stuck his head inside the car. "Because of my profession, no one is putting restraints on me, and I'm not sure I could do it to someone else in the bedroom, even if they were willing." He leaned closer. "But that doesn't mean I don't have a saucy side."

Biting down on the inside of her cheek, she did her best to keep from giggling.

"Yeah. I heard how that sounded. Go ahead, smirk, chuckle, get it all out. Whatever. I chalk it up to not sleeping for the last twenty-four hours." He slammed the door shut and jogged around the hood. He slipped behind the steering wheel.

"I've never been inside a police car before." It was a lie, but this was different and the excitement outweighed the fear. The only thing she had to be frightened of was the fact that Emmerson had the ability to make her feel things she had no business feeling. She might have to leave before she'd previously decided.

Three months might be just long enough to lose her heart to a man, especially to someone like Emmerson.

"It's a basic sedan with a few modifications."

"Does it go faster than a normal car?"

He glanced over his shoulder and backed out of the driveway. "Do I need to worry about you being a little speed demon?"

"Not once have I ever been pulled over."

"That doesn't mean you don't go too fast. I know all about radar detectors and those apps that warn people about my kind."

"Well, I don't have one of those radar things, but I do use that app. Mostly to alert me about traffic and accidents."

"Right. Likely story." He put the car in drive, palmed the wheel, and eased down the street. He turned down the police radio and tapped a button on the computer screen. "Just don't text and drive. I'll let someone go for a first speeding offense, as long as it's not in a school or construction zone, and it's not something insane, like a hundred miles an hour on the highway. I can be forgiving about rolling through a right on red once. But I see you with a cell in your hand, I'm done."

"Is there a story behind that?" Once again, she wanted to know everything. Every detail. She didn't want him to leave out one little thing about his life, including his work.

He nodded. "Four teenagers coming home from homecoming six years ago were hit head-on by some idiot sexting with his girlfriend. I fucking lost it when I read his text message and the timestamp. He could have waited or pulled over to tell his girl what he wanted to do to her. It was really graphic and gross. And wordy. My own mother had to pull me off him and suspend me for a week because I broke his nose."

"He kind of deserved far worse."

"He's still in prison and will be for a long time, but that won't bring those four kids back or ease the pain their families feel." He smacked the steering wheel.

Reaching out, she rested her hand on his thigh, squeezed, and then left it there. "I don't know how you do it."

"I don't know who that was harder on. Me or Jameson. I was the first officer to respond and the scene was straight from a horror movie. But Jameson and his crew had to pull those kids from the wreckage. Three were gone, but one had a weak pulse. The paramedics took over, but it was too late." He flicked the blinker on and pulled into the back parking lot of the Safe Harbor Café. Taking her hand, he kissed it. "I'm sorry. I have to stop dumping shit like this on you. It's too heavy."

"Maybe it's me who needs to stop asking the questions." She smiled weakly. "Thanks for the ride."

"Let me get the door for you."

"That's really not necessary." She grabbed his arm. "This time I'm insisting."

"All right, but kissing you in the front seat of my

vehicle won't be as comfortable as it would be out there."

"Not going to happen." She leaned over and kissed his cheek. "I'll see you later, Mr. Saucy."

He groaned. "You're not going to ever let me live that down, are you?"

"Never." Of all the places she'd lived, Lighthouse Cove was by far both the best and the worst.

Three months would be dwindled down to two.

Or maybe one.

Emmerson might not be the kind of man who would hurt her, but he was the kind of man who would run off with her heart.

5

Emmerson paced in the station's hallway while Emmett finished taking Rumor's statement. She'd already met with the sketch artist, but that hadn't produced good results, even though she'd tried her hardest to pull that memory from her brain. His mother actually had to admit that Rumor had given it her all.

For his entire life, the station had been a second home. As a small boy, he used to love to come visit his mother. She'd been a beat cop back then, but she was a proud deputy and loved her job. Her aspiration had always been to be the chief of police and she'd worked damn hard to get there.

Emmerson remembered fondly the day his mother's dream had come true. It had been a happy day in his house. His father bought a cake and pulled everyone out of school early. They had a massive party with friends and family. All Emmerson had ever wanted to do was be like his mother. To serve and protect the community in which he'd been raised.

His cell vibrated.

Rhett.

"Hey, brother, what's up?" Emmerson asked.

"I've got a few more things on Rumor and you're not going to like one of the things I found," Rhett said.

Emmerson pinched the bridge of his nose. This morning he thought he needed space. Time alone with his thoughts. That's why he'd gone to the dock. Of course, that was always where he went to think. But what he really needed was a friend. Someone to listen without judgment and that's exactly what she'd done. She was more than a breath of fresh air. "I'm listening."

"I found her last foster care family situation. It wasn't the greatest. But the disturbing part is one of the other kids who was living there with her at the time was a young man by the name of Tony Angelo. He went to prison about six months after he aged out of the system for having a suitcase full of drugs. They tried to pin a murder on him, but they didn't have enough evidence to do it. He was due to be released seven years ago, but shit went down in prison that tacked more years on his sentence. He got out six months ago."

"Okay. That's not a connection I want to hear, but

that doesn't mean Rumor and this Tony idiot were friends."

"Nope, but you have to admit, that's a little too close for comfort and I want to dig deeper."

Emmerson sighed. "Yeah. Just let's not poke a bear we can't put back in a cave."

"One more thing," Rhett said. "This Tony guy, he's up and disappeared."

"Fuck. I don't like the sound of that."

"Nor do I, but if I were you, I'd keep all this information from our mother. At least for now. She's not a suspect. And this has no bearing on the case."

"Unless you connect Tony to Tom Hemming's drugs. Then it might be a different conversation and I need you to look for that connection."

"Agreed," Rhett said. "What about Emmett? Nathan?"

"I'm not ready to loop them in yet. Too many cooks in the kitchen, if you know what I mean."

"Look at you being a rebel." Rhett laughed. "When Mom finds out, she's going to sit your ass to the sidelines. Without pay."

"I'm getting kind of used to it," he said. "I can deal with Mom's wrath. I just don't want my brothers pissed off. Those few years with Jameson after he found out Steve was his biological dad were pure fucking hell."

"The worst. I'll be in touch." The line went dead.

Emmerson let out a long slow breath. His brothers were his lifeline. His father, the voice of reason.

His mother? Well, she was his boss. He took orders from her and did the best he could to make her proud.

He loved her with his whole being. And he knew she loved him back.

But sometimes, she could be a real pain in the ass.

His mother stepped from her office with that confidant swagger that came from being a cop for over three decades. She was as tough as nails, and while she had a soft side, she rarely chose to show it. "You need to go home and sleep."

"I will as soon as Rumor's finished."

"I don't like her living in your pool house." His mom folded her arms and leaned against the wall. His mom was a force to be reckoned with. She had the best resting bitch face of anyone he knew. She was direct and never held back her opinion. As a boss, he valued and respected her. She knew when to follow the letter of the law.

And when to bend them.

As a mother, she'd been strict and tough. She demanded her boys stay out of trouble, which had proved impossible for all of them. As the chief of police, she had a reputation to uphold, and being seen as weak or soft wouldn't help her lead her deputies or keep the community safe.

"Other than her being in the wrong place at the

wrong time, I don't understand why." But truth be told, he knew the why. Any good cop would. However, he did want to hear his mom's perspective and the only way to get the honest answer he desired was to push the right button.

"The timeline," his mother said. "I can't believe you haven't connected those dots."

He ran a hand over his unshaven face. God, he hated that and if he didn't shave soon, he'd look like a buffoon. "If you're talking about the chatter of a new drug dealer making waves in Miami last month and us finding some of that cocaine in our town about the same time Rumor rolled in and how she stayed in that very hotel, that fact hasn't gone over my head."

"You know how I feel about coincidences."

"I don't believe in them either." He raised his hand. "But there are a dozen people who stayed there and two of them besides Rumor have spent time in Cali. I also have her employment record along with every known address she had in the last five years. She's never been anywhere near Tom Hemming and her record is clean. The only thing she's guilty of is bad timing and a shitty childhood."

"Tom's originally from California. Same as Rumor. That gives me enough reason to be concerned. And you should be too."

"There's more than one person from that state living here and don't start in on the timing again. I hear you. I understand your hackles are up. Mine are too. I've read the intel on Tom and it's not good. But two days ago, you trusted Rumor enough to bring her into your home and suggest I take her out."

His mom glanced down the hallway. "I follow my gut and it tells me she's not a drug dealer or a criminal."

"So, what's the problem?"

"The thing you don't want me to keep bringing up."

He sighed. The one thing his mother had always told him was not to ignore the simplest of details. It was those things that tripped up even the best cop. And she had a point. The day those drugs landed on the streets of Lighthouse Cove had been the day after Rumor had shown up.

"I'm not going to continue to lecture you," his mom said.

"Good."

"But I want you to stay observant and whatever you do, keep your dick in your pants until this thing is over. After that, you can take her to bed."

He smacked his forehead. "Ma, really? Besides me being a grown-ass man, do you really need to put it that way?"

"Sometimes I think it's the only thing you boys understand." She reached out and squeezed his biceps. "If she hadn't been from Cali, hadn't rolled into town when those drugs showed up, or hadn't been staying across the street when the murder occurred, I'd still be trying to fix you up with that girl. But until this case is put to rest, I'm not only asking you as your mother, but telling you as your boss, to keep a safe distance."

"I'll keep it professional." He held his mother's gaze, praying she didn't see right through the fact he'd already crossed the line. A single kiss wasn't a big deal. But now that he'd done it, he wanted more. Rumor was intoxicating. Addictive. And he couldn't put her out of his mind if he tried.

"Something tells me that's going to be impossible." His mother sighed. "Just be careful." She arched a brow. "Crossing streams makes things complicated."

Emmerson rubbed the back of his neck. He understood and respected his mother's concern, although he didn't view it quite the same way. Maybe he should. Maybe he was letting his emotions cloud his better judgment. It had been a long time since a woman had turned his head and made him want to do anything other than have a good time.

His cell phone buzzed.

He pulled it out of his back pocket and groaned.

Edwina: *I heard about the murder. I know how tough this must be for you right now. I thought I'd stop by later with a nice home-cooked meal. You never take care of yourself when you're on a big case.*

He rolled his eyes like a toddler. That woman sure knew how to get under his skin without even trying. In the few years he'd been with Edwina, the only *big case* he'd ever worked had been the one that ended their relationship. No fucking way would he respond. He'd already told Edwina he wished her well, but they had nothing left to discuss.

Ever.

But that hadn't stopped her from trying.

He told himself that if he ignored her, she'd give up.

"What's going on?" his mother asked. "You look like you swallowed a lemon and it made you constipated."

He might as well fill his mom in on what was happening because he wasn't sure it was going away. He lifted his cell and handed it to his mother. "If you want to be disgusted, you can read the text chain. You'll notice I've only responded once to tell her to stop."

His mom glanced between his phone and him while rolling her finger over the screen. "Jesus. Why didn't you bring this to me sooner?"

"I honestly thought she would get bored. Find someone else. Go away. I don't know."

"This is harassment and it makes me wish I hadn't been so kind to her all those years ago." She handed the phone back. "You should respond, telling her not to show up. Screenshot it and send it to me. If she does, file a formal complaint."

"I'm not sure I want to do that."

"You're being too soft," his mother said. "Besides,

a restraining order isn't a big deal. All it will do is set a tone and give me and your brothers the power to arrest her if she doesn't stop."

Emmerson sighed. "If she shows up, I'll go that route."

"You won't have any witnesses or proof you asked her to stop."

"Christ, Ma. I know the law. I get how this works. I'll handle Edwina." He cocked his head. "I won't let it get out of hand, but I'm not going to toss my badge in her face. You asked what the text was and I opted to be honest. In the scheme of things, Edwina is the least of our problems."

"That woman is always a thorn in my side." His mother squeezed his shoulder. "Deal with her or I will." She ducked back into her office.

Fuck. The last thing he needed was his mother going all mama-bear on him, but that's exactly what she'd do the next time she crossed paths with Edwina.

Emmerson: *I won't be around later. Please don't stop by. And please stop texting. I've made my position clear. Don't make me use my office to make it clearer.*

That should get rid of Edwina and also keep his mother off his back. He tucked his cell in his pocket and leaned against the wall.

Rumor emerged from the last office down the hallway with Emmett one step behind.

"I need a minute with my brother. Why don't you

go to the lobby. Emmerson will meet you there," Emmett said.

Emmerson cocked his head. He held his brother's stare, trying to get a read on the situation, but Emmett gave up nothing.

Neither did Rumor.

"I need the ladies' room," Rumor said.

"You'll see it on the way out." Emmerson squeezed her arm. He watched her backside as she made a beeline toward the other side of the building. "What's going on?"

Emmett raked his hand through his hair and glanced toward the ceiling. He always did that during a case when something didn't fit, but it stood out. "The statement she gave is the identical story she gave you, Chris, and Mom."

"Don't tell me you're now believing Rumor could be involved in this drug ring with Tom Hemming?"

"God, no. And Mom doesn't either. But you know her. She gets something in her head and she won't let it go. I have to admit the timing does have me on edge."

Emmerson glanced over his shoulder. "I'd be lying if it didn't give me pause. However, I ain't going to say that to Mom. She'd run with it."

"She already is." Emmett nodded. "I'll be straight with you, because Mom won't."

"Fucking wonderful." Emmerson shook his head. "She had you interview Rumor not because she thought I was incapable of separating work from having Rumor rent my pool house, my attraction for her, and being a good cop, but because she wanted you to either trip her up or get something else out of her." He inched closer. He might be the younger brother, but he could be just as intimidating. "What did Mother want to know and why didn't you tell me before you conducted the interview?"

"I don't need to answer the latter because you know why and you would have done the same thing in my shoes," Emmett said with a tight jaw and frustration dripping from every syllable. "This wasn't to see if Rumor was lying. Ma absolutely believed her story. Every piece of it. This was a routine statement, which you could have taken." Emmett let out a long breath. "But Mother thinks—and I have to concur—that Rumor is holding back something. She was nervous as fuck. Twitchy. She constantly played with her hair. Or her leg rattled a mile a minute. Answering the questions was easy, but being here wasn't. And she doesn't do small talk well."

"Would you in this situation?"

"Probably not," Emmett agreed. "But this wasn't basic nerves. This was the behavior of someone who has something to hide. I can't pinpoint it, because again, it wasn't the questions that made her uncomfortable. Her story jibes no matter how we asked the questions. It was the process. It was as if she thought at any moment there could be a shift in the discussion and I'd be breaking out the handcuffs and slapping them on her wrists."

"Honestly, that could be more to do with the concept that Mom had you do the interview, and not someone she was more comfortable with—me."

"I thought about that and I would normally agree had I not met her before the party or spent any time with her at Mom's house," Emmett said. "It's something for us to consider moving forward on this case. And something I want you to think about since she's living in your pool house."

Part of Emmerson wanted to lay into his big brother. Tell him to fuck off. But that wouldn't do him any good. Besides, Emmerson had one ex-girlfriend who resorted to criminal behavior.

And another one who was cheating right under his nose.

His track record read like a rap sheet.

"I appreciate you keeping an eye out for me." He squeezed his brother's shoulder. "I'm taking all of this under advisement and keeping Rumor at arm's length."

"For some reason, I seriously doubt that." Emmett arched a brow. "Just promise me you'll be careful."

"I always am." Until he got his heart broken.

All Rumor wanted to do was go home and take the hottest shower possible. She'd done what she could to remember every detail possible of the night in question. She wanted to help Emmerson in his investigation. She desperately wanted him to solve this murder and would do her part as a good citizen. To make up for what she couldn't have done all those years ago.

That last thought made her want to cry and laugh at the same time.

For fifteen years she'd done what she could to put the past in the rearview mirror. To be a good person.

But she'd witnessed her boyfriend kill a man in cold blood and she'd done nothing.

It didn't matter that the man in question was a drug dealer. He was still flesh and blood.

And now, because of her inaction once again, someone else was dead.

She stared into the mirror as she gripped the sink to keep her hands from shaking. This was her worst nightmare.

Taking out her phone, she googled the murder and scanned the few articles.

Heather Green found murdered.

Heather had moved away from Lighthouse Cove ten years ago, but recently returned six months ago. She had a record that included drugs, sex trafficking, and dealing. She'd been living in the motel for the last month.

But the article didn't say anything else.

No other names had been mentioned.

The article did cover the fact that the police had few leads except a new drug runner from Miami but didn't mention their name either.

She dropped her cell into her bag.

"Get ahold of yourself. You did nothing wrong. You gave a statement. You have nothing to worry about. This has nothing to do with you." She squared her shoulders and stepped from the bathroom, making her way into the lobby.

"Hey, Rumor," a male voice called.

She glanced over her shoulder.

Nathan. Another cop. Another brother.

"Oh. Hi," she said, smoothing down the front of her jeans. "How are you?"

"Hanging in there. Sorry we had to drag you down here. How'd things go with the sketch artist?"

"I wasn't much help," she admitted.

"We appreciate you trying." He smiled. "Where's Emmerson?"

"Talking with Emmett back there." She pointed. "I was told to wait in the lobby, but I think I'm going to go outside for some fresh air."

"I don't blame you. I'll let Emmerson know that's where you are."

"Thanks." She made her way through the main doors. The hot, humid Florida air smacked her face. Closing her eyes, she let her skin soak up the sun's rays. Flashes of when the police had found her living alone flooded her brain. The questions. The fear of being taken from her home. Child protective services. Her first night in foster care. It all came crashing down.

"Rumor?" Lucy Ann's voice lulled her to the present. "Are you okay?"

Rumor blinked. "Yeah. I'm fine."

"What are you doing here?" Lucy Ann asked.

"I had to give a statement about what I saw at the motel."

"Ah." Lucy Ann gave her a weak smile. "The whole town is on edge about that. I'm so sorry that you're being dragged into it. If you need any time off, just let me know."

"That's not necessary. Besides, I didn't see anything useful."

For Emmerson's sake, she wished she had and that thought confused her because it would only complicate things for herself and she wanted no part of this investigation.

"How is Emmerson holding up?" Lucy Ann asked.

That was an odd question and she wasn't sure how to answer. "He's tired."

"I'm sure he is." Lucy Ann nodded. "He takes these kinds of things to heart, especially when he knows the victim."

Rumor jerked her head. "He didn't tell me that."

Lucy Ann sighed. "I'm not surprised. It's not like

any of us have spent any time with Heather since high school. She has always run with a tough crowd. His mother picked her up twice before we all graduated and three more times after that. I'm pretty sure that Emmerson has slapped cuffs on her as well before she moved away. Heather had a troubled childhood. Her dad was a real loser and her mom wasn't much better. Poor Heather barely stood a chance. But it wasn't like Rebecca didn't cut her break after break when she was a teenager. I'm sure Emmerson is taking it hard. As if he could have done something to prevent her death, when there was nothing at all. If Heather wouldn't give up the drugs or the lifestyle, his hands were tied."

Rumor actually understood that. Tony not only lived to do drugs, but the greed had gotten to him and he wanted the bigger piece of the pie.

"Thanks for telling me that. I understand a little better why this case has Emmerson so tied in knots."

"There's that and the fact that Emmerson is just one of the good guys. He's kind, generous, and has the biggest heart. He hates to see anyone hurting. Even the Heathers of the world. He tried to help her, just like he tried to help that ex of his, Edwina. She's a real piece of work." Lucy Ann leaned closer. "If you ever cross paths with that one, don't believe half of what comes out of her mouth. She has her sights set on Emmerson again, and she'll lie, cheat, and steal to get him."

"I'm sure he's smarter than that."

"Oh, he is. But she doesn't care who she hurts in the process." Lucy Ann smiled. "And a little birdie told me that Emmerson is quite smitten with you."

"Smitten?"

"Yeah. You know. Has a case of the hots for you."

Rumor's heart did a little tango in her chest. It was an unwelcome sensation. But worse, her lips curved into a smile.

"Glad to see the feeling's reciprocated."

"I said nothing of the sort." She did her best to frown.

"You didn't have to." Lucy Ann winked. "Speak of the devil." She took off up the stairs. "Emmerson, you look like shit. And you really need to shave."

"Gee, thanks. It's nice to see you too." He paused to give Lucy Ann a peck on the cheek. "What are you doing here?"

"Heather had been in the café the day before the murder. Your mother wants a statement."

Emmerson ran his fingers through his hair. "She didn't mention that to me. Was Heather with anyone?"

"She came in alone. When three different people came to her table, but didn't stay, I knew what was going down and asked her to leave. She gave me a hard time, but I told her I'd call the cops if she didn't."

"What did she do?" Emmerson asked.

"She paid her bill, cussed at me, and walked out the front door. I stood there and watched her get into a nice SUV with a man behind the wheel." Lucy Ann held up her hand. "I didn't get a plate. Not for lack of trying. And I didn't recognize the man, nor did I get a good look. All I can tell you was that he had shoulder-length dark hair. I couldn't even tell you his age."

"Why didn't you call me? Or one of my brothers?"

"I couldn't prove what she was doing—"

"Lucy Ann. After everything that went down with Trinity, you should have called us before even asking her to leave. We all know she's bad news. It doesn't matter that we were all once friends."

Oh. That was interesting.

"I get it and you don't need to lecture me. I got enough of that from Phil. It won't happen again. I feel bad enough she's dead."

He squeezed her arm. "That's not your fault."

"Doesn't mean I won't regret my decision, even if I couldn't prove what she was doing." She waved her hand. "I watched the scene and I didn't see anything passed between her and the people who came to visit. No envelopes. No money or drugs that I saw. They weren't regulars. Or townspeople. Trust me, I watched them like a hawk and all I saw was conversation."

"All right. Thanks for letting me know," he said. "Say hello to Phil and the kids."

"Get some rest before you fall over, and for the love of God, shave. Facial hair is not a good look for you." Lucy Ann patted his cheek.

He laughed. "I will." He jogged down the last few steps and placed his hand on the small of Rumor's back. "I take it you heard that conversation."

"Kind of hard not to when I'm standing two feet away," she admitted.

"I hate to ask, but were you working that shift? Did you see what she was talking about?"

"I was not there." Thank God for small favors.

"I need you to do me a favor and be very quiet for this conversation." He pulled open the door to his personal vehicle before sliding behind the wheel. He tapped his cell and set it in the cradle.

"Hey, Emmerson. I'm about to head into a meeting. What's up?" Rebecca, the chief of police and his mother, asked.

"You mean an interview with Lucy Ann? About the case that I'm supposed to be leading?"

"You're tired and need to sleep."

"Not the point. You should have told me."

"I'll send you the report when I'm done," Rebecca said.

"Are you going to pull me off this case? Because if you are, I'd prefer to know that now."

"Where's Rumor?" Rebecca asked.

"Waiting for me by my car," he lied right through his teeth.

Something Rumor wouldn't have expected from him and she wasn't sure how she felt about that.

"Look," Emmerson said. "Rumor mentioned Heather was fighting with a man. Lucy Ann is the only other person to mention Heather with a man. I wanted to—"

"Cut the bullshit, Ma. Either you know something I don't and are choosing not to share it with me. Or you don't trust I can do my job. Or both. So, just be straight with me."

"All right. You and Heather have a history," Rebecca said.

"Going to the sophomore dance together isn't a history. It was two dates when I was a dumbass kid rebelling against authority, which happened to be my mother. And if you're going to bring in my other exes and how all that turned out, I'm going to march my ass right back into the station and be part of that interview."

"You've got a lot coming at you, especially with this thing with Edwina. That was disturbing to say the least and I'm not happy with how you're handling it."

"Seriously? That's why you pulled this stunt?"

"Yes," Rebecca said. "And it wasn't just what you showed me. That woman has been—"

"Not another word, Ma. I'm dealing with it and you better not meddle. Got it? Now, what else do I need to know that you're keeping from me?"

"Nothing," Rebecca said. "But this has gotten

personal for you and I know how you get. Go home, Emmerson. Get some sleep. We will regroup tomorrow."

"Later, Ma." He tapped the screen and yanked the gear shift. "Thank you for being quiet."

"You're welcome, but I wish I hadn't heard any of that."

"Family politics." He chuckled. "My mother thinks I'm soft. She always has. And part of her is right. Even if I ever wanted to be chief, I'd suck at it. Nathan is the best man for the job. He's got my mother's balls."

Rumor covered her mouth.

"No. Go ahead and laugh. Even my dad says that Mom has a bigger set. She had to in order to make it in her profession. But sometimes it's frustrating as hell to be her son. I didn't take this job to be an asshole. To push my badge in people's faces. I want to do good. To help and protect people. Not go around arresting every idiot who makes a mistake, and that included Heather. I just wish she hadn't come back and made the same stupid decisions."

Never in her life had she met a man as passionate as Emmerson. Or as caring. She reached out and placed her hand on his knee. It was a bold statement. But something told her that he needed someone—anyone—to have his back. "Being soft doesn't make a man weak. It just means you can see both sides of a coin. That's a gift that most people aren't capable of."

"Believe it or not, my mom has it too. She really can have a big heart. She just can't show it."

"I rest my case."

He took her hand and kissed it. "You're good for my soul."

Rumor wasn't so sure about that, mostly because she was going to haul ass out of town the second she got her get out of jail free card.

She would become another one of those women he hadn't been able to read properly and that broke her heart.

6

There was nothing better than a good thin crust pizza with extra cheese and meat. Top that off with an ice-cold beer and a beautiful sky as the sun disappeared behind the bridge, creating a combination of blue, red, and orange colors, out on the pool deck, and well, Emmerson couldn't think of a better way to spend his evening.

Except now he got to share that experience with Rumor.

He twisted open one of the beers and set it on the table in front of her before pulling out one of the chairs. "While we don't actually get the sunset, you still can't beat the view."

"No, you can't," she said softly, lifting the cold beverage and taking a swig. "This is a completely inappropriate question and I'd understand if you didn't answer. But how on earth do you afford this place on a cop's salary?"

"That's a valid question." He opened the pizza box and served her a slice before digging in for himself. It wasn't the first time someone questioned him on his purchase. Most believed his mother and Steve either gave him a loan or even bought it for him. Same with Jameson. Especially Jameson, since most people in town didn't take into consideration that Jameson's wife had a thriving business and Jameson was the town handyman.

Neither man corrected anyone. They didn't give a shit what anyone thought.

"I've lived a humble life. Outside of a home I owned for two years with a woman I lived with ten years ago, I've always had small apartments that didn't cost much. My brothers accused me of being a minimalist. I suppose I couldn't deny that, but I'm too old to live in a garage apartment anymore."

"The upkeep on this place has to cost a small fortune." She waved her hand toward the waterfront. "And that boat. I can't imagine the price tag for that."

He laughed. "Miles and I own that sucker together. And as far as the rest of it. Well, it's not so bad. I don't go out much and I've saved over the years." He stuffed his mouth full of the best pizza in town. Maybe the state. After he was done with his meal, he would have to call it a night. His mind was barely functioning from lack of sleep. Every muscle was sore and weak. As much as he wanted to sit and chat with Rumor for hours, even his bones demanded rest. "I imagine it's been hard for you to save, moving from one town to the next. One job to the next."

"It has, but I still wouldn't trade it for all the money in the world." She lifted her beer to her rosy, plump, kissable lips. She was like no other woman he'd ever met. She was an onion. Her layers needed to be peeled back one at a time. And like an onion, she had a strong and powerful presence, but she wasn't for everyone.

That's what he liked.

But the cloud hanging over her head that he knew was filled with a dark secret both intrigued him and made him take a step back. It wasn't that he believed she could be involved negatively in this case.

Quite the contrary.

But it triggered something and he needed to peel those layers until he found it.

"I'm curious. Do you think you would ever find a place that would tame the wanderer in you? Have you ever given it a consideration?"

"When I first left California, my plan was to travel for a few years. See the country until I found the right spot," she said, wiping her fingers on a napkin. Her nails were cut short, and even though she wore no nail polish, they were well manicured. This evening, she wore her long hair in a ponytail at the nape of her neck and he wanted to free the strands. "But the more

I move around, the more I think there isn't that perfect place for me, or I haven't found it yet."

"Lighthouse Cove is a nice place. I hope you'll stay awhile."

"I enjoy living in the moment, taking things one day at a time. It's easier that way. Less stressful."

"I would think it would cause more anxiety," he said. "Not having solid roots would make me twitch. I like structure."

"That's an overrated concept and a crutch." She tapped her beer against his.

"Maybe. But it's stable. It allows for long-lasting friendships." He stared at the hummingbird tattoo on her wrist. No color. Just black ink. But the three-inch tattoo was exquisite. He reached out and traced the tiny wings. "Is there a story behind this tattoo?" He pointed to her bare feet. "Or the other three on your ankles? They're very interesting. I like them all."

"Thank you." She smiled. "The butterfly was the first one I got. It was about six months after I left California. It represents freedom and change from a past life. From being in foster care and not being seen or heard." She twisted her leg, showing off another tattoo. "I've always loved dolphins and evenings. And dolphins are so calming."

He wanted to comment that moving around as much as she did made her closed off, never forming true bonds with people.

But that would be rude.

"I take it you like to read and drink whiskey." He leaned over and lifted her leg, resting it on his lap, tracing the image with his finger. Her soft skin ignited a fire deep in his gut. It wasn't that he'd sworn off relationships. He hadn't. But he had made a promise to himself that he wouldn't jump into the deep end. That he would take his time getting to know any woman who turned his head.

"I developed a taste for bourbon when I spent a few months in New Orleans and when I was living in Nashville, I found other whiskeys to enjoy. Books have always been my jam." She leaned back, taking another swig. "They gave me comfort when I was living in foster care and felt as though I had no one."

"I'm sorry you had to experience that."

She shrugged. "While it's a part of who I am, I refuse to let it define me. In some ways, it helped shape me into an independent human, capable of taking care of myself."

"It's a good quality to be able to turn a bad experience into a positive."

She leaned over, tugging at his shirt, boldly exposing his chest. "Tell me about this?" She traced her fingers over the bear tattoo on his right pec, sending a warm tingle through his system.

Sleep might not actually come if this continued.

"Me and my brothers all have one and my mom has a mama bear with seven cubs on her ankle. We got them after she and Jameson made peace with each other."

"That's nice."

He opened his mouth but was cut off by the damn doorbell.

Rumor jerked. Her foot hit the pool deck with a thud.

Yanking his cell from his pocket, he checked the door app.

Fucking Edwina.

Aggressively, he set his cell face down on the table. "Un-freaking-believable," he muttered. He shoved his plate aside, snagged his beverage, and chugged, but he didn't budge.

"Aren't you going to get that?"

"Nope," he said. "She'll go away."

"She?"

He closed his eyes and concentrated on the hum of a motorboat buzzing by. The sound did nothing to settle the nasty pit that had formed in his stomach. Every time he'd run into Edwina, she'd find a way to touch his arm or shoulder. She'd let her fingers linger on his body. It made him want to crawl out of his skin. He honestly wished her well.

As long as she stayed away.

He could forgive.

But he couldn't forget.

It wasn't that his heart was broken. Not by her. Not anymore.

He blinked.

"Edwina." There was no emotion attached to her name. Only apathy with maybe a little pity mixed in.

This town had a long memory and people still talked. As much as his mother had tried to protect her from the backlash, most had learned what had happened. It was in part the reason she left Lighthouse for greener pastures.

She'd tell it was because of some great opportunity and not because she'd been part of a sex scandal. Although, the news reports never quite made it clear what role she'd played in the sex trafficking ring.

"Do you mind me asking who exactly she is and why we're ignoring her? I mean, I've sort of heard who she is, but it's not only mean to blow her off, but a little childish."

"She's the first real girlfriend I ever had. We were in our early twenties. Young and stupid. She moved away after we broke up and just recently moved back to town. She doesn't understand boundaries or the fact I have no interest in her or any residual feelings left."

"You did not just say residual."

He chuckled. "I absolutely did and she's one big fucking royal pain in my ass."

"Emmerson? Are you back… there you are." Edwina pushed open the pool gate and strolled across the pool deck carrying a casserole dish. She wore a sundress with thin straps. The neckline plunged low, showing off her cleavage. Her breasts bounced up and down as her hips swayed back and forth. It was hard not to look. Even Emmerson had to admit she was sexy.

However, her personality and past grievances ruined it.

"Oh, I didn't know you had company," Edwina said, setting the dish on the table. She scowled, staring at the pizza box.

"The extra vehicle parked in the carport should have been the first clue," he mumbled.

"I left you a message telling you that I'd bring you dinner."

"I wanted pizza." He guzzled his beer. Thank God he had an outdoor fridge because in about five minutes, he was going to need another. "And I also thought I made myself clear about stopping by when I texted you back." He held Edwina's gaze with an arched brow. "While I do appreciate the thought, I'm busy. I don't mean to be rude, but it's been a very long two days."

Edwina pursed her lips and turned her attention to Rumor. "I don't believe we've officially met and since Emmerson is feeling prickly, let me introduce myself. I'm Edwina. Don't you work at Safe Harbor Café and the trinket shop?"

Rumor nodded. "It's nice to meet you." She stretched out her arm. "The name's Rumor."

"That's a unique name. Is there a story behind it?"

"My parents were big Fleetwood Mac fans," Rumor said.

"Interesting." Edwina leaned over the table, pressing her hands on the ceramic top, pushing her breasts together. "So, do you live around here?"

"That's none of your business," Emmerson said. "Do you mind? We're on a date."

"A date? That's a shocking revelation." Edwina pursed her lips. "Is this some kind of joke?" Edwina asked.

"No. Thanks for dinner," Emmerson said. "You shouldn't have, and I mean that in the sense that I don't want you to do it again."

Edwina stiffened her spine, folding her arms and heaving her breasts upward.

If that was supposed to get his attention in a sexual way, it didn't work. All it did was remind him that while he cared about Edwina at the base level, he had no emotional ties to her at all.

None.

Zero.

Zilch.

"Someone needs to take care of you because you won't do it for yourself." Edwina inched closer to Emmerson, placing her hand on his shoulder.

He shrugged it off. "I manage and I have Rumor here now."

Edwina glared. "Emmerson, walk me to my car. I'd like a moment alone to speak with you. It's important and I'd prefer to do it in private, if you know what I mean."

"Actually, I don't. And you've crossed a million lines. Don't cross another one," Emmerson said.

"We need to talk."

He laughed. "We have nothing to say to one another."

"It will only take a few minutes," Edwina said.

"We're not doing this. I've asked you nicely to stop this. Don't push me to make this a police matter. No one wants that. Not even me."

Rumor rested her hand on his thigh. Immediately, a warm sensation flowed through his body.

She was an anger whisperer.

And a good one at that.

"It's time for me to call it a night. Thanks for the beer and pizza," Rumor said.

He grabbed her hand. "Edwina is the one who is leaving and we're finishing our conversation."

"It won't hurt you to escort her to—"

"She made it back here by herself. She can return to her vehicle the same way," he said calmly. Emmerson threaded his fingers through Rumor's, lifting her hand and kissing the back side. He shouldn't have. It was a dangerous game he was playing with his emotions. But he'd do anything to get Edwina off his back and out of his life. He could handle running into her. He could even be nice. However, not when she behaved like a stalker.

Edwina jerked out her hip, planting her hand on it. "Well, I can take a hint. Enjoy the dinner I made you. The heating instructions are taped on the top, as you can see." She, and her fancy heels, marched off toward the side path.

Rumor glanced over her shoulder. "You weren't very kind," she whispered. "And we're not on a date."

"She's facing harassment charges as it is."

"Are you kidding me?" Rumor snapped her gaze back to Emmerson's. "For being neighborly and bringing you food. Talk about throwing the weight of your badge around. I'm shocked you'd be like that." She ripped her hand away.

"You don't know the whole story." He stood and made a beeline for the outdoor fridge, snagging two beers. "That's not the first time she's shown up unannounced. And she's been texting me. Relentlessly. I won't even get into the things she says to me because if I did, I'd need to go take a shower with bleach."

"Don't shoot me, but could you have done something to give her the wrong impression?"

"Absolutely not." He handed her a second beer. "In an attempt to ensure we could pass each other on the street and not cause a scene, I met her out for coffee when she first came back to town. It was a half hour conversation where I told her all was forgiven. It was then she started making advances and I put her off. What happened between us was a long time ago and she's not a person I want to be involved with. Ever. I have made that crystal clear. She won't stop."

Fuck. This was the last thing he wanted to talk about.

Fucking Edwina.

He couldn't wait for Rumor to meet Tessa. Not.

At least Tessa didn't want him back. No. She hated him and she had a good reason.

His cell buzzed.

He glanced at the screen.

Edwina: *I didn't deserve that in front of a stranger, especially when we had plans. I know it's because you're tired. Please call me tomorrow.*

"For fuck's sake," he mumbled. "I'm sorry. I'm exhausted and I'm not firing on all cylinders." He was going to have to file that restraining order first thing in the morning. This couldn't continue. He didn't want to use his position, but she left him with no choice. "I'd like to show you around town. Or maybe take you for a boat ride. I've got some work I need to do tomorrow morning with the case, but then my mom has given me a little time off. Unless something comes up. Do you have plans tomorrow evening?"

"I work in the gift shop in the morning, and then I'm covering lunch at the diner. I'm off at four."

"How about we meet back here and I'll take you for a boat ride."

She glanced over her shoulder as if to consider the proposition.

"We might see a dolphin."

"Now that's something I'd love to experience." She pushed back her chair and stood. "All right. I'll see you then. Can I help you clean this up?"

"You don't have to do that."

"I want to." She rested her hand on his biceps.

"I guess I can't say no." He smiled before folding the pizza box.

She collected Edwina's dish, which he planned on tossing. "Do you want that? Because I'm not going to eat it."

"Seriously?"

He pulled open the sliding glass doors that led into the white and gray kitchen that his sister-in-law, Brie, had helped design. It was gorgeous, but it didn't belong in a bachelor pad. When he cooked, it was generally on the grill, or he used the microwave to reheat things he snagged from dinners with the family. He'd been a bachelor for so long, and making meals for one had become slightly depressing.

Not because he wanted a wife, but because he didn't want to spend the time. The one thing he and Tessa did enjoy doing together was putting meals on the table. It had been fun. It was the only time they laughed.

Otherwise, they were always fighting.

"Damn. This place is gorgeous." She set the dish on the island and ran her fingers over the dark-blue leather sofa. Another thing Brie had picked out when he bought the place. Who was he kidding? Brie and all his sisters-in-law had a hand in helping him decorate. If it had been left up to him, he'd have a folding table in the kitchen and a beanbag chair in the family room.

"Thanks." He placed the leftover pizza in a container and shoved it in the fridge. "I wasn't joking about whatever is in that thing." He waved his hand over the island. "I'm not eating it out of principle. But you're welcome to it."

"Now I'm afraid she might have poisoned it."

He tossed his head back and laughed. Hard. "That would be Tessa, not Edwina."

"And who is she?"

"A woman I lived with for two years about ten years ago. It wasn't a great relationship and it ended even worse. She has a pretty poor opinion of me."

"Now I'm really intrigued. Why?" Rumor plopped her cute little ass on one of the stools and rested her chin in her palm.

"To make a very long story short, we started out strong until she wanted to move in together. I didn't think we were ready. I wasn't ready. I was still traumatized after Edwina, and Tessa knew it. I wanted to wait." Emmerson leaned against the counter, taking another swig. He had no idea why he chose to share his ugly, sordid romantic past. It certainly didn't make him look like good dating material with a woman he wanted to spend more time getting to know. But there he was, babbling on about it. "However, because I did care for Tessa and wanted her in my life, we started looking for houses. No sooner were we in than the talk of marriage crept into our daily conversations."

"I take it you weren't ready for that either, and she wanted a ring on her finger."

"Like yesterday." He laughed. "But to be fair, it wasn't like I didn't think about it. We were living together. I wouldn't have done that if I didn't believe we had a future."

"So what was the problem?"

He raked his fingers through his hair. "I have some trust issues stemming from my relationship with Edwina." He raised his hand when Rumor opened her mouth. "I don't want to talk about it."

"Alrighty."

"Anyway. I didn't see why we had to rush into anything. I figured we could enjoy living under the same roof for a year or two, but Tessa didn't like that. All her friends were getting married and having these big elaborate weddings. And kids. Boy, did she want kids."

"And you don't?"

"I did back then," he admitted. "But I wasn't in a hurry for them. She was and it started to grate on me and I handled it by working double shifts."

Rumor sat up taller. "Oh, I'm sure that didn't go over well."

"You're right, it didn't. As a matter of fact, I came

home between shifts to find her in bed with someone I used to call friend."

"Ouch."

"Hence, I still have trust issues with women."

"I don't blame you. I would too if I were you." She slid from the stool. "Which is why I value my lifestyle. I answer to no one but myself. I'm free to come and go whenever I choose and I don't have to yell at anyone for not putting down the toilet seat."

He burst out laughing. "My mother raised seven boys. That was her biggest pet peeve."

"I can't imagine one human coming out of this body, much less seven. Your mom's a saint."

"Not really." He looped his arm around her waist. "I'll walk you to the door."

She jerked her head. "Seriously? I can't imagine what could possibly happen to me in twenty paces."

"You could fall in the pool and I can't let that happen."

She patted his chest. "You can watch me and make sure I get in safely."

In that moment, he realized how much he didn't want the night to end. He didn't care how exhausted his body was or how desperately he needed sleep. He wanted more time with Rumor. It had been soured with Edwina's presence and all this talk about his past love life.

Curling his fingers around her wrist, he pulled her tight.

She tilted her head and gazed into his eyes with a mischievous look. "What are you doing?"

"Kissing you goodnight," he whispered right before landing his lips on her mouth. He kept it soft. Delicate. Teasing her before deepening the kiss, swirling his tongue around hers in an exotic dance. He couldn't get enough, but he didn't want to take too much. Or come on too strong.

Rumor was special.

Even with the dark cloud that hung over her like a storm at sea waiting to unleash. She had a past. Everyone did. Whatever she hid behind those sweet eyes, he was sure it couldn't be some terrible secret.

But the reality was, it could be.

He broke off the kiss. "Walk home safely."

"Should I text you when I get there?"

"Good idea." He smiled.

She shook her head, stepping through the sliding glass doors. "See you tomorrow afternoon." She waved her hand over her head.

Leaning against the doorjamb, he watched her hips sway back and forth. A woman who moved every year? Either she was running from something.

Or hiding from it.

His hackles should be standing at attention.

"Lock the doors," he called.

"Do I need to be concerned about you sneaking in during the middle of the night?"

"Trust me. If I wasn't so in need of a good eight

hours, I might not be behaving so gentlemanly right now."

She pulled open the door. "Something tells me that's the only way you know how to behave." She disappeared into the pool house. "But I hope you'll shave by tomorrow, because that stuff on your face isn't doing you any favors."

He sighed, locking the slider. The moment his head hit the pillow, he'd be sound asleep.

Dreaming of his sexy tenant.

7

For the next hour, Rumor tossed and turned on that damn comfortable Murphy bed. She tried watching one of her favorite television shows, but it did nothing to soothe her soul.

Or rid her thoughts of Emmerson and his lips.

Next, she tried a book.

But she'd read a line or two and couldn't remember what she'd read.

So, she went back to the TV, trying a new show. However, it didn't hold her attention.

She decided some fresh air might help.

Not bothering to change from her pajamas, which were a tank top and boy shorts, she stepped out onto the pool deck with her book in hand, making a beeline for the big comfy sofa.

"Hey, you," Emmerson said.

"Jesus." She skidded to a stop. "You scared the fuck out of me."

"Sorry." He chuckled. He'd been sprawled out on the sofa with a glass of something in his hand. He shifted, making room. "Can't sleep?"

"Nope." She eased onto the couch and lifted the bottle from the coffee table. "I see you and some really good tequila are having a party." She smiled. "And you shaved."

"I got tired of all the women in my life making rude comments about it." He laughed, waving the glass. "I thought this might help me take the edge off since I've been rolling around in my big bed, unable to get that shut-eye I need so desperately."

"Mind if I take a shot?"

"Help yourself." He handed her the glass.

"Thinking about the case?" She polished off the drink, giving it back to him.

"That's one thing that's on my mind, but honestly, I'm not sure it's what's keeping me up tonight." He poured more into the small tumbler and took a sip. "You see, there's this woman living in my pool house and she's wormed her way into all my thoughts."

"I'm not sure what to say to that."

"Me neither." He reached out and tucked some of her hair behind her ear. "I've been sitting here for the last forty minutes contemplating texting you. Or knocking on the door. Every time your lights go on, I stand up and make it halfway there. But then the lights go off and I take that as a sign."

"Now who's being a stalker."

"That's not even remotely funny." He cocked his head, but his lips formed a slight smile.

"Come on. It is a little."

He chuckled. "What's your reason for not being able to sleep?"

She took a big old shot of courage. "It might be something similar to you."

"Might be? That doesn't stroke this old man's ego much."

"You're not old and I doubt your ego needs much stroking."

He set the glass on the table. "You'd be surprised."

She met his gaze, feeling a rush of emotions she'd spent a lifetime trying to avoid. She never wanted a man in her life. Not one that she cared this much about, and how did that happen in just a few short days? It made no sense. "Maybe we both just need someone to keep us company tonight," she said softly.

Emmerson's eyes softened as he leaned in closer, his breath warm against her skin. "I don't want just anyone's company," he murmured, his hand reaching for hers. "I want yours."

Her heart raced as their fingers intertwined, a silent understanding passing between them. Without another word, he closed the distance between them, capturing her lips in a gentle yet urgent kiss.

Time seemed to stand still as they lost themselves in a thunder of passion, the world fading away until all that existed was the electricity crackling between them. And in that moment, all her worries and doubts melted away, leaving only the undeniable pull she felt toward Emmerson.

She should run. She should leave Lighthouse Cove behind, making it a distant memory. Staying would only delay the inevitable. Emmerson was the kind of man who loved with all his heart and she wasn't the kind of woman who stayed in one place.

"Let's take this inside," he whispered.

In a moment of weakness, she stood up and followed him into the house, her heart pounding in her chest. He'd been open with her about his past loves. His past heartbreaks. And she had no right to join him in his bed when she knew damn well she'd leave.

Emmerson led her to his bedroom, the air so thick with anticipation and desire she was drowning in it.

Once inside, he turned to face her with longing in his dark eyes. Without a word, he reached out and traced the line of her jaw with his fingertips, sending shivers down her spine. She let out a shaky breath as he leaned in to capture her lips in another searing kiss. No man had ever treated her with such tenderness. Such love. And she barely knew him.

She tried to remind herself that they were ships passing in the night. That he understood she had no intention of making this sleepy little town her home, but that did nothing to ease her soul.

Or her heart.

Their hands roamed each other's bodies, seeking solace and connection in the heat of the moment. Clothes were shed in a frenzy of desire until they were both consumed by the raw need for each other.

In that intimate space, stripped bare of pretense and barriers, they found comfort and passion in each other's arms. She couldn't help but wonder if he only needed a body and she was the closest one around. He'd been through so much in the last couple of days.

But what about her and what she'd been through? He knew nothing of her struggle. He knew so little of her past and what brought her to Lighthouse Cove to begin with. But that was her plight, not his. It was her burden to carry and he had enough on his plate. She could absorb his for one night.

As they made love, she couldn't help but feel a sense of guilt and shame. She knew that he deserved better, and she had to admit that she was not the one to give him what he truly needed—a life partner, someone who could share his joys and sorrows, someone who understood the weight of his responsibilities and the countless lives depending on him.

But for now, she clung to the moment, the warmth of his skin, the rhythm of his breath, the beating of their hearts as they merged into one. She hoped that this one night of connection would be enough to help them both forget the pain that was creeping up on them, the shadows of their pasts, and the uncertainty of their futures.

Afterward, they lay entwined, their breaths mingling, their bodies still pulsating with the aftermath of their passion. He whispered softly in her ear, "Thank you. That was… something special."

She smiled, tracing his lips with her finger. "You're welcome."

They lay there in silence for a few minutes, savoring the warmth and intimacy they'd shared. But eventually, reality began to seep in and she knew soon enough it would be time to face the music. Time to leave. Time to break his heart.

Emmerson cupped her cheek in his hand, his eyes filled with a mix of gratitude and sadness. "I know you have a wandering soul," he said, his voice barely above a whisper. "I understand. I just hope you'll stay in my town for a long time. I like you."

"I like you, too." She wrapped her arms around his strong body and closed her eyes. But she wouldn't stay. Not long anyway. Her days were numbered. She didn't know how long. She couldn't pack and leave with the investigation going on. That wouldn't look good and the last thing she needed was to be hunted down by the police.

God, as much as she couldn't look at Emmerson and call him a mistake, staying would be.

8

R umor leaned against the counter. The lunch crowd had dwindled down to almost nothing. She glanced at her watch. Thirty minutes before her shift was over. She'd heard nothing from Emmerson all day. The fact that he'd slipped from the bed without her knowing or saying goodbye bothered her.

It shouldn't. But it did.

She had no claim to him and last night was a fleeting moment. Two people who needed a connection. She had worried he might read more into it, but she wondered if she hadn't meant anything at all, and that was troubling for a different reason.

She felt a little better when she made her way to his kitchen and found a note. She pulled it from her apron and unfolded it.

Rumor,

Sorry I had to sneak out. Duty calls. I'll be in touch later. Help yourself to coffee, breakfast. Anything you need. Here is a set of keys. Please lock up when you leave. I'll be in touch later.

Emmerson.

The front door to the café dinged and two women strolled in. She tucked the note back in her pocket. She stiffened her spine, smoothing down the front of her apron. "Welcome to the Safe Harbor Café."

One of the women smiled as she looked Rumor up and down with a narrowed stare. "You're new." What an odd thing to say.

"I am. Just the two of you today?" Rumor asked.

"Yes. And we'd like that booth over there." The woman pointed to the corner booth.

"Not a problem." Rumor snagged two menus and showed the women to the table. "I'll be right over with—"

"We want two waters. No ice. With lemon. We also want two of Phil's special lemon drops. Thank you," the woman said as she eased into the booth. She had long blond hair, styled with big curls. She wore way too much makeup, but it went with her pricey shoes and designer clothes.

"Sure thing. Coming right up." Rumor set the menus on the table and turned. She paused a few paces away and smiled. Though that quickly turned into a frown when she realized Emmerson was in uniform and he didn't appear to be all that happy. "What are you doing here?"

He leaned in and kissed her cheek, letting his glorious lips linger for longer than what would be deemed appropriate. "I need food and coffee."

"Take a seat anywhere. I'll get that coffee right after I take care of—"

"Emmerson, we need to finish our conversation. You hung up on me and that wasn't nice." The woman barreled past Rumor.

"I called you about something else and you never let me get it out. I don't want to talk to you about your wedding or help you with Ben and Sarah," Emmerson said.

"Come on. I know you and Ben are friendly these days."

"I'm not getting involved." He let out an audible sigh. "I'll take a seat at the counter. If I wasn't so damned tired and starving, I'd leave."

"Sounds like you've had a day." Rumor curled her warm fingers around his biceps. "I'll get you that coffee."

"I can't believe you won't do this for me. It's not like I'm asking you to—"

"Tessa, the answer is no. Go back to your booth and let me be. I've had a shit few days." He climbed up on one of the stools with his strong shoulders slumped.

Tessa scoffed, turned on her three-inch designer heels, and stomped back to her booth.

Rumor gathered the waters and put in the ladies'

drink orders. Since the café wasn't busy, the drinks would take only a few minutes, so she decided to pour Emmerson his coffee and give him what she assumed was some much-needed attention. "Are you okay? I don't mean to pry, but you look as though you lost your best friend."

"Stuff like this is never easy." He ran his hand across his unshaven face. "You're going to hear about this soon enough, so it might as well come from me."

"What's wrong? What happened?"

"There was another murder," he said softly, closing his eyes for a moment. When he blinked them open, a tear fell. He quickly wiped it away. "Edwina."

"Oh no." She grabbed his hand and squeezed it tight. Not only for him, but for herself. "When?"

"I won't know the exact time of death until we get the autopsy report and that could be awhile. But sometime after she left my house and four in the morning when I got the call."

"Shit. I'm so sorry. I know you and she didn't have a good relationship, or even a friendship, but I do know that you cared."

"Thank you for that." He lifted the mug and blew before taking a sip. "I feel like shit because of the way she left last night. If I had known those would have been the last words I spoke to her, I would have never said them."

"You had no way of knowing." Rumor took his hands. She could feel the pain flow from his skin to hers and it tore through her system like a runaway freight train. "You have to remember she crossed a line."

He let out a curt laugh. "You're the one who told me I wasn't nice." He lowered his gaze.

"I didn't know the whole story when I said that. Look at me."

He lifted his gaze.

"First, what she was doing to you was definitely harassment. You know that and you also know you let it go on too long. She left you with no choice but to be harsh. And second, what happened isn't your fault."

"I know that, but it still doesn't make me feel any better." He lifted her hand and kissed it. "Thank you for trying, though."

"Um, excuse me," Tessa called, waving her hand. "When you're done flirting, would you mind getting us our water and drinks."

"I'll be right back." She patted his hand.

"You can tell Tessa to fuck off," Emmerson said, and not softly either.

"I heard that," Tessa said.

Emmerson turned, glancing over his shoulder. "I called you a little while ago not because of Ben and Sarah. But instead of letting me tell you what happened, you gave me a fucking earful."

"You were giving me a warning," Tessa said.

"Not about that," Emmerson said. "But since

we're on the subject. Leave Ben and Sarah the fuck alone; otherwise, it will become a police matter."

"Using foul language isn't necessary." Tessa pursed her lips. "And I have no idea what you're talking about."

"Yeah, you do. And if it happens again, they will be calling me in an official capacity, not as a friend."

"Are you threatening me?" Tessa lifted her chin.

"Consider yourself warned." He palmed his mug and muttered a few obscenities under his breath. "And both you ladies please be careful. Lock your doors and be aware of your surroundings. You'll understand more of why I said that when you watch the news tonight," he said in a softer tone. "Call me or 9-1-1 if you see anything suspicious."

"Is this because of what happened to Heather?" Tessa asked.

Emmerson nodded.

Tessa held his gaze for a moment before turning her attention back to her friend.

"I can't tell if you hate her or still care about her," Rumor said.

"It's a little bit of both." Emmerson shrugged.

"You're a good man." Rumor snagged a tray and placed the drinks on it. She made her way across the room and set the drinks in front of Tessa and Stacey. "Here you go, ladies. Do you know what you want?"

"Yes. We do," Tessa said. "I'll be having the summer salad."

"I'll do the same, thank you."

"Coming right up." Rumor turned, but Tessa grabbed her arm.

Rumor glanced down at the fingers curled around her wrist. "Is there a problem?"

"Woman to woman," Tessa whispered. "Watch your back when it comes to Emmerson. While even I can admit he's a decent human, he's not boyfriend material. He'll break your heart into a million pieces."

"I don't need advice from a woman I don't even know." Rumor jerked her arm free. She didn't care if Tessa and her friend left her a shit tip. Or no tip. No one put their hands on her for no reason. "And don't touch me again."

Tessa lifted her hands. "Hey. Just trying to give you fair warning. But if you want to learn the hard way about the kind of man he is, well, that's on you."

"The man has had a rough day. Give him a break."

"That's the problem. His job is all he cares about. It sours every relationship he's ever had. It will happen to you too."

Rumor leaned a little closer. "Trust me. I know all I need to about Emmerson. And about you too." She tapped the engagement ring on Tessa's finger. "I just hope for your fiancé's sake, you don't cheat on him too." Rumor turned on her heel, held her head high, and made her way back behind the counter. Fuck. She shouldn't have said that. It wasn't her place, but she hated cheaters. A woman she worked for back in Knoxville had a husband who had an affair and watching what she'd gone through had been rough.

"I've lost my appetite. You can cancel our order." Tessa stood, slapping some money on the table. "You sure know how to pick them, Emmerson. And you love to tell people only one part of our story, leaving out the things you did."

"For the record, he didn't pick me. I chose him," Rumor said. "Don't let the door hit you on the way out."

Emmerson chuckled.

"Glad I amused you," she muttered.

"And me too." Lucy Ann appeared from the kitchen carrying a plate with a cheeseburger and fries. "That woman is a bitch and I heard she got engaged to the guy she was cheating on Ben with."

"I saw the rock. It was big. Gaudy actually," Rumor said. "Who's Ben?"

"An old friend," Emmerson said.

"He used to be your best friend until that witch got her claws into him." Lucy Ann placed the plate in front of Emmerson. "I just heard what happened to Edwina. I'm so sorry. I didn't like her or what she did to you, but she almost wasn't as bad as that one." Lucy Ann pointed toward the door. "The way she used your career to justify her being lonely and cheating was pathetic."

"She's not wrong," Emmerson said. "At the end of our relationship, I was never home."

"Why do you always cut her a break?" Lucy Ann glared. "Tessa wanted you to leave the police department. So did Edwina. That's unfair. All you've ever wanted was to be a cop."

Emmerson laughed. "Let's remember why Edwina wanted me to leave."

"Okay. I don't want to speak ill of the dead, but what did Edwina do and why would she want you to stop being a cop? I only ask because I know what Tessa did. I get her reasons. She wanted you in a nine-to-five position. And honestly, I'm not liking her much because what she said to me was a see you next Tuesday move."

"That's a nice way to call her what we all think of her," Lucy Ann said. "And, Emmerson, you might as well tell Rumor because it will be on the news tonight. Your mom can't contain this shit show."

"I know." Emmerson nodded. "But not on an empty stomach. I've had a shit day."

"Take all the time you need, Mr. Saucy." Rumor smiled.

Lucy Ann arched a brow. "That needs some explaining."

"No. It does not." Emmerson took a massive bite of his burger.

"Well now. I think I have my answer." Lucy Ann disappeared back into the kitchen.

"Sorry. I was just trying to lighten the mood. It just came out."

Emmerson caught her gaze. "I don't care. But you might because my mother is coming to my house in a couple of hours to have a conversation with us both."

Rumor glared. "Why would she do that?"

"Because I had to tell her that I was with you all night."

"Jesus, why would you do that?"

"She got an anonymous tip from someone saying they saw you and Edwina fighting at one in the morning at Lucky's Bar. But we both know that's impossible."

"But it's my word against whoever gave this tip."

He took her hand. "No. It's our word and mine carries a lot of weight in this town."

She swallowed. Hard. "Yeah."

"I know what you're thinking."

"I doubt that," she said softly.

"The real question is why does someone want to set you up? Because that brings me to the second tip we got."

"I don't think I want to hear this."

"Someone told my mom it was you fighting with Heather before she was murdered."

"But I didn't even know—"

"Relax. We all know this is bullshit. We just have to find out why someone in this town has it in for the new girl."

"Easy for you to say. You're not the one coming under fire." She wiped her hands on her jeans. How the hell did this happen? What on earth had she done to anyone in this town? Her pulse pounded in her ears so loudly she could barely hear herself think.

"Nope. I'm not. But I am taking what's happening personally." He dunked a fry into some ketchup and plopped it into his mouth. "Someone is trying to redirect this investigation by having us focus on you. Whoever it is doesn't know where you spent the night last night. It's why I've asked some of my brothers to come over before my mom."

"Seriously?" She glared. "Which brothers?"

"Rhett and Miles."

"Fucking wonderful." She smacked her hands against her thighs. "I get to be interrogated by a cop and two private dicks. Just how I wanted to spend my evening."

He lowered his chin and arched a brow. "You're being dramatic."

"And you're belittling how I feel right now."

"I'm sorry. I don't mean to. But not a single person in my family believes you had anything to do with this. However, we do need to figure a few things out. My brothers and I want to get a jump on it because my mom can be intense."

"You don't understand how triggering this is for me. What it brings back from when I was taken into foster care." While she could never tell him about

Tony or what had happened, she had to give him something to sink his teeth into. Something that would justify her nerves. Her fear.

Emmerson wiped his hands on a napkin and leaned back. "I will make sure we keep that in mind. But can you tell me a little about that so we can be sensitive to it?"

"I don't like talking about it."

He nodded. "Hey, Lucy Ann," he called. "Do you mind if Rumor clocks out a little early?"

"Nope. She's all yours, Mr. Saucy." Lucy Ann stuck her head out of the kitchen.

Emmerson shook his head. "You can't call me that. Ever." He reached around the counter and took Rumor's hand. "Come on. We've got a little time before my family gets to my place."

She snagged her bag and followed him out the door. "Cop car again," she mumbled.

"Did something happen between you and the police that has left a bad taste in your mouth?" He leaned against the hood, pulling her between his legs and tight against his chest. He kissed her softly. It was sweet. Tender. It wasn't a passionate kiss, but a caring one and it wasn't something she was used to. Most men she became entangled with only kissed her when they wanted to end up in the sack. The only intent behind this was to show he valued her and that he cared.

"Yes," she admitted, caving to the sensation that

she'd successfully avoided her entire adult life. If she didn't allow anyone too close, she'd never be hurt again. She'd never feel the pain of abandonment. Of betrayal. She could go through life with a sense of contentment and that was enough. But Emmerson made her want more and she found herself for the first time willing to share things she never had. "I lied about ever being in cop car." She pressed her hand over his mouth. "It was when I was placed in foster care. I was young and scared. The police were all very kind. It's not that I'm afraid of cops. But I didn't want to go with them. I wanted to stay home, where I'd been living on my own for weeks. I knew for sure my parents would be home and I wanted to wait for them. Sometimes, even now, I wonder if they ever returned."

"How long had you been alone? How old were you?"

"Eleven and I think it had been close to six weeks."

He cupped her face, kissing her tenderly. "That kind of trauma sticks with you. I'm sorry. I can't imagine what that was like for you. Have you ever tried to find your parents?"

She shook her head. That would require putting herself out there and that meant it was possible Tony could find her. That, she couldn't have.

"Why not?"

"Fear, I guess."

"What are you afraid of?"

"Learning they never came looking for me at all."

He cupped her face, resting his forehead against hers. "That's reasonable. I'd probably feel the same way. But if you ever want to, I'd be happy to help you."

"Thank you," she whispered.

"However, I can't leave my work vehicle here. I have to drive it home."

"I understand. I do. I don't mind being in it. Or with you. It's the rest of this that has me unnerved."

"Trust me. I'm not thrilled with the situation either. I didn't like having to tell my mother what happened last night. Or anyone else. That's between us. But I've got two murders on my hands. Both women I went to high school with. One I took to a dance and one I dated for over two years and thought I was madly in love with. I tried to speak with Tessa about my concerns for her safety today, but all she cared about was me getting involved in something between her and her ex-husband."

"Ex-husband?"

"Yeah. The man she cheated on me with, she married. He and I used to be best friends and we're working our way back into a friendship, especially since Tessa slept with and now is engaged to his stockbroker. It seems to be a pattern with that girl."

"If she's with someone else, why is she bothering this man and his new girl?"

"Because she's an event planner. The best in town and she won't take on Tessa's wedding out of principle and now she and Ben feel like they are being harassed, which they kind of are."

"Jesus. Can I go get some popcorn? This is better than *Real Housewives*."

He chuckled. "My life reduced to reality television."

"I'm sorry. That was rude."

"No. It was funny." He batted her nose. "Come on. My brothers are probably waiting." He pushed from the car and opened the door. "But if you start calling me Mr. Saucy in front of them, it will actually stick and we don't want that."

"We? Or you?"

"I don't mind it." He winked. "But can you handle being called Mrs. Saucy this early in the game?"

"Fuck no." She fastened the seat belt. Boy, was she in way over her head. But what she struggled with the most was she liked it. She stared out the window. Of all the places she'd lived, she still liked Lighthouse Cove the best. The streets were filled with kind souls. People who greeted her with a smile and a friendly word. Even with everything that was going on, this sleepy seaside town sang to her heart. "Do I need to be prepped for this meeting?"

"A little bit." He pulled into his neighborhood. "I want you to know that I would have done this no matter who you were and I started the process only because you were renting my pool house."

"Why do I get the feeling we're about to have our first official fight?" She gripped the door handle, ready for her fast getaway.

"At least I know we're something official."

"I wouldn't go that far." She shifted her gaze as he rolled to a stop in his driveway. "What did you do?"

"A background check."

"You're an asshole," she muttered.

"No. I'm a landlord well within my legal rights. I just didn't go about it the way normal people do and used my brother Rhett to dig into your background." He held out his hand. "Before you storm off. Almost all of what we found is shit you basically told me. However, there are a couple of things we need you to connect the dots on and only because we want to keep you safe from whoever is killing people and trying to frame you for the crime."

"Excuse me while I don't feel as though you're on my side right now." She tugged on the handle.

He reached across the vehicle, holding her biceps. "I get you're pissed. I probably would be too. But I need your help. And I also need to keep you safe." He cocked his head. "Not to mention that I care about you."

"You don't know me." She shoved his hand away. "You think you do because you read some file on me and slept with me. But you don't. Now, I need to go change my clothes before you and your brothers rip my life apart." She jumped from the front seat, glancing over her shoulder as the first of his brothers arrived.

She raced around the side of the house with her entire body shaking. Emmerson had checked into her past. He knew things. Maybe he knew about Tony. Other things.

Shit.

Lighthouse Cove was no safe harbor. Not for her. It had turned into her worst fucking nightmare dressed up in a sexy cop layered in betrayal.

Emmerson slammed the driver's door of his police car shut. He pinched the bridge of his nose. So much for being honest.

"You look like shit," Miles said.

"I feel worse."

"The case? Or problems in paradise?" Miles leaned against the hood of the police car. He was two years younger and looked more like their mother with his light hair, light-brown eyes, and thinner frame.

But he had their father's contemplative demeanor.

Miles would have made for an excellent police officer and for years Emmerson tried to get him to join, but Miles wanted nothing to do with the so-called family business. He rebelled more than anyone else in the family against being a cop. Even more so than Rhett and Jameson. Or even Seth, who had followed in their father's footsteps and became a lawyer.

In their mother's eyes, that was as honorable as being a cop, except Seth sat on the opposite side of the law, defending criminals, which always made for interesting conversation at the dinner table.

When Rhett had decided to become a private investigator, even though he'd studied to become a police officer, their mother had flipped out. She struggled with the career mostly because private investigators got in her way. But she warmed to the idea when Rhett aided her in a few investigations, doing things she couldn't do because the law had tied her hands.

Jameson was always given a pass in part because firefighting was a first responder job. But mostly because Jameson wasn't her first husband's biological child and their mother had so much guilt over that one it damn near ate her alive.

But Miles had chosen to become a mechanic and their mother had no idea what to do with that.

Of course, he worked part-time with Rhett, taking on some PI cases, but that wasn't good enough for their mother.

"Both," Emmerson admitted. Everyone in his family knew he'd spent the night with Rumor. There was no getting past that fact. His love life was none of their business, but because of recent events, it had become a family problem. He trusted his brothers and he needed their help more than he needed his badge.

"I take it you read through what Rhett and I found."

"I skimmed through the important parts."

"What are your thoughts?" Miles asked. "More importantly, do you believe Rumor has anything to do with this Tony guy or even Tom Hemming and his drug business?"

Emmerson scratched his scruffy face. He hated not shaving. He once tried to grow a beard and it lasted all of two days. Glancing at the sky, he stared at a big puffy white cloud as it passed over the sun, as if it held all the answers he needed. This was by far the toughest case he'd ever worked on in his entire career. Not only because it involved two murders of women he knew, but because it now appeared to involve another woman he'd grown to care for in a short period of time.

He'd always been the kind of man who fell hard and fast. Edwina had been his first love and he had loved her with all his heart. Her betrayal had nearly destroyed him as a man, and as a police officer. For years, he found himself questioning his ability to perform his job effectively.

And his love life?

Nonexistent.

But not for lack of trying.

Until Tessa.

He tried to take his time getting to know her, but his heart demanded more and he caved, even though his mind forced him to hold back. Maybe the failure of their relationship was on him, something he struggled to come to terms with, but if he were being honest, he'd loved her too.

And there were other women he'd loved. However, he could never fully allow himself to trust.

He wanted so desperately to believe Rumor was different. Special.

"Until I speak with her about it, I'm not making any judgments." He shifted his gaze, catching his brother's, daring him to pick a fight.

"You haven't said anything to her about it?"

"Not about Tony or Tom. Only that I dug into her past. She did not respond well to that."

"Would you?"

"I'm a cop. What's to find in my past?"

Miles laughed. "Um, I could name a few things. Like when Mom busted you for streaking."

"Don't be an ass. You know what I mean," Emmerson said. "I've always known Rumor was hiding something. She's been moving from town to town for fifteen years. Who does that?" He held up his hand. "Either someone who is running from something. Or someone who is…" He let the words trail off. He couldn't even say them out loud because he didn't believe them. Not one little bit.

"Yeah." Miles rested his hand on Emmerson's shoulder. "Based on her past, what she went through, and her history of moving around, I'd say she's hiding and running."

Emmerson arched a brow. "You're giving her the benefit of the doubt?" The sound of an engine pulling down the street caught his attention. He turned his head.

Rhett pulled into his driveway.

"I am. She left California when she was eighteen. When Rhett and I checked into drug running in the towns she'd lived in since then, we never found anything like this. No major drug running. Nothing associated with her name. The fact that Tony was released six months ago and is now missing and Tom is in Miami, makes both Rhett and I think either she has something on them or—"

"They have something on her," Emmerson said.

"That's not what I was going to say." Miles shook his head.

Rhett stepped from his SUV. "Why are we standing out here?"

"Because Emmerson here is letting his mind go to some deep and dark places," Miles said.

"Of course he is." Rhett gave Emmerson a good slap on the shoulder. "Let's go find out what your girlfriend has to say."

"She's not my girlfriend," Emmerson muttered.

"Yeah, right. And my wife's not pregnant." Rhett gave Emmerson a good shove. "Whatever the actual connection Rumor has with these men is, I doubt it's as bad as that cop brain of yours is thinking."

"I'm just tired of women lying to me." He squared his shoulders and strolled toward the front door, unlocking it.

"You should change out of that uniform," Rhett said. "You don't want to intimidate the poor girl."

"And don't bring your gun," Miles added. "We'll see you poolside."

Emmerson made his way to the master. He stared at the bed, which she'd made. He sighed as he shed his uniform and found a pair of shorts and a T-shirt. Pulling out his cell, he texted Rumor, telling her that his brothers were there and to meet them by the pool.

She responded immediately.

Rumor: *I'll be out in a minute.*

At least she wasn't ignoring him.

When he stepped from the sliders, she had yet to come out from the pool house. He joined his brothers at the table, taking the beer they had pulled from the fridge.

"How do you want to handle this?" Rhett asked. "Do you want us to start with what we found?"

"No. It's best if it comes from me." He took a hearty swig and stared at the door.

Minutes ticked by before Rumor emerged wearing a pair of jean shorts, a tank top, and no shoes. She'd taken her hair out of her ponytail and it flowed over her shoulders. He much preferred that look.

Without saying a single word, she pulled out a chair and folded her arms across her chest.

Not a good sign.

Rhett offered her a beer.

She shook her head.

"Look. I get you're mad," Emmerson said.

"Mad is an understatement, but go ahead."

Emmerson rubbed the side of his face, wishing he'd taken the time to shave. "I've got a real drug problem in this town right now and—"

"And you think I have something to do with that?"

"No," he said quickly, interrupting her because deep down he believed that. Needed to believe that. "But someone in your past—"

"You only know things about my past because you went digging. You have serious trust issues," she said.

"Are you going to keep interrupting me? Or are you going to let me speak?" He glared.

She waved her hands.

Thankfully, his brothers sat quietly, sipping their beers.

"Yes. I went digging. I'm a cop. I'm renting my pool house. I wanted to know who was going to be living in my backyard. Do I believe you're involved with this person? No. But you were in the past and I need information on him and I want it now before my mother gets involved."

"If you think this is uncomfortable," Miles said. "Our mother will be worse."

Emmerson rolled his neck. "You were in foster care with Tony Angelo. What can you tell me about him?"

"Not much," Rumor said. "We lived under the same roof for a couple of years. He got into a lot of trouble and I did my best to stay clear of him and his buddies." She crossed and recrossed her legs three times in those two sentences.

She wasn't telling the whole story.

Fuck.

What the hell was she hiding and why?

"What kind of trouble?" Rhett asked.

"Drugs. Stealing. You name it, he was into it," Rumor said. "But I haven't seen or heard from him in years." She held Emmerson's gaze and didn't blink once.

Truth.

Good.

"What about Tom Hemming?" Miles asked.

"I don't recognize the name." Rumor folded her hands in her lap and stared at them.

"You've never heard of him?" Miles asked.

"I can't say that I have." She didn't look up.

Lie.

Fucking A.

Emmerson gulped his beer. He wanted to stand and pace, but he needed to continue to gauge her response. He needed to have cop instincts, even if killed him.

This next round of questions was going to be one hell of a conversation and Rumor was either going to lie or get up and leave. Or worse, kick him under the table. "Your last known address in California matches—"

"Emmerson? Rhett? Miles?" his mother's voice boomed across the Florida air like nails on a chalkboard. "Are you back here? Is Rumor with you?"

"She's fucking early," Miles whispered.

"Her timing always sucks," Emmerson said. "Yeah, Ma. We're here." He stood.

His mother came barreling around the corner and his heart dropped to his toes.

"Tessa? Johnny? What are you doing here?" Emmerson asked.

Tessa walked with a limp and her arm was in a sling. "Jesus, Tessa. What the hell happened?" He raced to her side. He might have personal issues with the woman, but he did have a heart.

"Hit and run," his mother said. "It could have been a lot worse. Thank God, Old Man McCurdy was there to push her out of the way."

Emmerson ran his hand up and down Tessa's good arm. "I'm so sorry and I'm glad you're okay." He stretched out his arm and shook Johnny's hand. The only beef he had with the man was that he slept with a married woman. "Did we get a plate? A description of the driver?"

"No plate," his mother said. "We got a description

of the car, the driver, and a passenger, but it doesn't add up."

"Why not?" Emmerson asked.

"The car is the same make, model, and color of Rumor's vehicle," his mother said.

"But I haven't used my car all day." Rumor jumped to her feet.

His mother raised her hand. "I know that, dear."

"What else am I not going to like about this?" Emmerson clenched his fists.

"I'll answer that," Tessa said. "I want to state that when we called the police, I made it abundantly clear that I knew without a shadow of a doubt it was not Rumor driving that car, but someone trying to pose as her."

Emmerson glanced over his shoulder.

Rumor stood there with her jaw tight and her eyes wide.

"Okay." Emmerson shook out his hands. "Please fill me in because I feel like I'm missing part of this story."

"When I left Safe Harbor Café with Stacey, we went down the street to Oscars and got a table outside. We watched you and Rumor get in your patrol car and drive off. I was so mad at you because you wouldn't help me, and her for what she said to me, that I didn't want to be out anymore. It was fifteen minutes later when I was hit. I knew it couldn't have been her." Tessa pointed. "Regardless of my feelings, I would never accuse anyone of wrongdoing. I'm not like that. Besides, the person driving the car was obviously wearing a wig."

"Um, while appreciate the fact you're defending me, how do you know that?" Rumor asked.

"I own a salon. I know these things and it was the worst wig I've ever seen," Tessa said.

"What about the passenger?" Emmerson asked.

"That's the worst part about this whole thing," his mother said. "According to Tessa here, the man was wearing what appeared to be a Lighthouse Cove police uniform."

"You've got to be fucking kidding me," Emmerson said.

Rumor went to sit back in the chair but missed it altogether and fell backward into the pool.

Splash.

"Shit." Emmerson raced to the side and dropped to his knees. He reached for Rumor, pulling her from the water. "Are you okay?"

"No," she said.

He lifted her out of the water and into his arms, carrying her to a chair. "Someone get her a towel, please."

Rhett jumped into action.

She wiped her wet hair from her face. "I think we need to talk about what I really know about Tony and Tom."

10

R umor stood in the middle of the pool house with her heart hammering in the center of her chest. She had no desire to be honest. To relive what had happened fifteen years ago and why she'd been running her entire adult life.

But this was no longer only about her.

People had died.

And now a good man was also being set up.

She couldn't allow this madness to continue.

If she ran, not only would Tony find her, but the cops would be looking too. That was no way to live.

Knock. Knock.

"The door's open," she said.

Emmerson stepped inside. "Tessa and Johnny are gone."

"I'm sorry she got hurt." Tears burned her eyes.

"It's not your fault."

"You don't know that because you don't know what I did." She glared.

He closed the gap between them, taking her into his arms. "You're right. I don't. But you didn't hit her with your car. You didn't murder two innocent people. Whatever happened in the past, you've been trying to put it behind you. What I need from you now is that truth and we can figure out what to do next."

"Even if that means you have to slap handcuffs on me?"

"I told you, I'm not into that kind of kinky thing." He winked.

"Not the time to be making that joke." She cocked her head.

He kissed her in that sweet, tender way he had that let her know he was on her side and she wanted to hate him for it. She didn't want him to care about her because she was only going to hurt him in the end.

She pushed him away. "Let's get this over with." She snagged the bag with all the money in it, minus what she'd earned on her own. That wasn't much, but it was hers and she wasn't going to part with it.

"What's that?"

"I don't want to have to explain this twice." She dragged the suitcase through the door and across the pool deck, doing her best to hold her head high.

Emmerson was one step behind her and he

managed to pull out a chair for her, being a true gentleman.

This time, she took the beer Rhett offered and chugged half of it. "Any chance I can cut some kind of immunity deal or something?"

"That's not something I have the power to do," Rebecca said. "But something tells me no matter what's in your past, you won't need it."

"I don't know how these things work, so I have no idea." Rumor kept one hand curled around her beer, and the other she rested on the bag of cash.

"If what you tell us is indeed criminal, and we have to take it to the next level, we know a couple of good attorneys and of course, we'll put in a good word," Rebecca said. "But again, we're getting ahead of ourselves."

"Not to mention what we dug up doesn't add up to you being arrested for anything," Rhett added. "We just need you to fill in the blanks so Emmerson and our mom can do their jobs."

Rumor nodded. "Can I just start talking without all the questions? It makes me nervous."

Emmerson took her hand. "Whatever you want." He kissed her palm.

Damn fucking man was too kind.

She sucked in a deep breath and let it out slowly. "So, we all know I lied about knowing who Tom Hemming is, but for the record, I never sold drugs for him. Ever. I wasn't that girl."

"We believe you," Rebecca said.

God, she hoped so.

"As I told you, I met Tony while I was in foster care. What I left out was that he was my boyfriend." Rumor swallowed the bile that smacked the back of her throat, but it didn't go down. It got lodged there and not even another sip of beer would make it go away.

"We gathered that when we learned you were living with him after you left the system," Emmerson said.

She cocked her head. "Please, just let me get through this without interruption."

Emmerson nodded.

"Tony lied to me when we first moved in together. He told me he was done with that life. That he had turned over a new leaf, but he hadn't. And he kept trying to pull me in. I knew I needed to leave, but I didn't have any money. It was an abusive relationship."

Emmerson growled. It was deep, low, and menacing.

"He would tell me we were going out to dinner, only we'd end up doing a drug run first. One day, we went to this guy's house. I had no idea that Tony planned on not only double-crossing this one dealer, but Tom as well. He killed the guy, right in front of me."

"Jesus." Emmerson squeezed her hand.

"I'm sorry you had to witness that," Rebecca said.

"It was the worst thing I've ever seen in my life. It came out of nowhere," Rumor said. "One minute they were talking, the next minute…" She paused, taking a deep breath and wiping the tears away. "Tony collected the drugs and the money. He was even the one to call the cops. He then called Tom and told him that he couldn't collect because the building was surrounded by the police."

"That's convenient," Miles said. "Did Tom buy it?"

"It was all over the news, so yeah. Besides, Tony was in tight with Tom." Never in a million years did she think she'd be sitting at a table with two cops and two private dicks, telling this story. But here she was and all she could think about was what cold metal might feel like around her wrists.

"What did you do?" Rhett asked.

She reached for the suitcase and opened it, showing off all the money she'd stolen from Tony. Or Tom, depending on how one looked at it. "Once we got home, I waited for Tony to pass out. I took the money, went to the corner, and made an anonymous call to the police about all the drugs Tony had and that I thought he might have had something to do with Ollie's murder."

"From your personal cell?" Emmerson asked.

"Yeah. But I broke it right after and tossed it so no one could track me." She blinked.

"That's smart and while Tom didn't have a big operation back then, he does now. And he's got crooked cops and politicians in his back pocket," Rebecca said.

"That's how they found out you made the call." Once again, Emmerson kissed her hand. "Tony went to prison because of that tip you gave the police." He pointed to the bag of money. "Neither he nor Tom care all that much about that cash. It's small potatoes to them these days. But they do care about what you did. They care about the fact you put Tony in prison and fucked with Tom's operation."

"But how did they find me? I've been careful. I don't stay anywhere for very long. I try to use cash and—"

"Same way we tracked your journey across the country," Miles said. "Thing is, Tom has been setting up shop in Miami for a while now. You simply made it easier for them by coming here."

"What happens to me now?" Rumor asked.

"In terms of what?" Rebecca asked.

"I was there when that man was murdered and I did nothing." Rumor tugged her hand free. She couldn't stand another second of Emmerson's kindness.

"Not that I ever want to see human life taken, but he was a bad man selling drugs. He's off the streets and Tony went to prison," Rebecca said.

"And the money I stole?" Rumor asked.

"What money?" Rebecca stood and closed the suitcase and zipped it shut. "I don't see any cash. You boys see any cash?"

"No, ma'am," Emmerson said.

"You listen to me, Rumor." Rebecca lowered herself and took Rumor's hands. "I've been a police officer since I was twenty-one years old. I trust my instincts. I know when someone is lying to me and I knew you weren't telling us the whole truth at times. I know you're telling it to us straight now. I get why you did what you did and if I were in your shoes, I might have done exactly the same thing. Right now, my job is to nail these bastards to the wall. Your job is to live your life without having to do it in fear. When you drove into town, there was a sign welcoming you to Lighthouse Cove. Do you remember what that sign said?"

"Everyone needs a safe harbor to sail into," Rumor whispered.

"That's right. And we're your safe harbor." Rebecca squeezed her hands. "There is nothing in what you told me that would make me want to haul you in for any kind of questioning or arrest you. All I ask of you now is that you don't leave town. That you work with us and let my son protect you because I'm ordering him both as his mother and his boss to stay at your side twenty-four seven until we arrest Tony and Tom and take down their drug ring. Deal?"

"I can do that," Rumor said. "I don't want to see anyone else die because of me."

"Don't let me ever hear you say that this is your fault again." Rebecca arched a brow. "Just because you're the one who pissed them off doesn't mean you're responsible. If it wasn't you, it would be someone else. Assholes like this don't need much of a reason to flex their tiny muscles and kill people." She stood. "Now, I have work to do." She turned her attention to Emmerson. "You're stuck to her like glue, got it?"

"Yes, ma'am." Emmerson nodded.

"I'll be in touch." Rebecca squeezed Emmerson's shoulder before marching off around the side of the house.

"Who was that woman and what did she do with our mother?" Rhett raised his beer. "Damn, that was wild."

"I like this side of Mom." Miles smiled. "Almost makes me want to be a cop and work for her."

Emmerson laughed. "Trust me, once this case is over, she'll be back to her old self."

Rumor leaned back, nursing her beer. She didn't know if she wanted to join in with the boys and laugh.

Or bury her head and cry like a fucking baby.

A phone buzzed.

All three men pulled theirs out.

"I'm out of here," Rhett said.

"Me too." Miles stood.

"Who texted you? Because I didn't get one." Emmerson frowned.

Rhett waved his cell in front of Emmerson. "Why, Mother, of course. She doesn't want us to overstay our welcome."

Emmerson stared at the phone for a moment. "Oh, for fuck's sake," Emmerson muttered. "Lucy Ann has a big fucking mouth and our mother is a piece of work."

"Later, Mr. Saucy." Rhett practically ran around the side of the house and Miles was on his heels. Both men were laughing so hard that Rumor couldn't help it, she laughed too.

"I'm glad you can find humor in something."

"Nothing about today has been funny." She waggled her finger. "Except that."

"Um, you falling in the pool was actually kind of hysterical."

"Now that's just kicking a girl when she's down." Rumor tilted her head. "Calling a man saucy, on the other hand, could be seen as a compliment."

"Not when it comes from their mother, and you didn't see the text." He smacked his forehead. "Stick around long enough and you'll find out just how embarrassing my family can be."

"Now I want to know what the text said."

"Nope. I'm not telling you that."

"Come on. It can't be as bad as the whiplash I have from this conversation. I mean, I've gone from being terrified of being arrested to… to… I don't know… being comfortable again. It's weird."

"Weird?"

"Do you have any idea what it's been like for me these last few days? It's not like I wanted to do this to you. Or keep all this shit from you. While I always worried Tony would get out of jail one day and find me, I didn't think he'd go on some killing spree, try to frame me for it, and then try to make the cop I was sleeping with an accessory." She waggled her finger. "And there's that part. I freaking slept with you."

"Because that's a bad thing?"

"I didn't say that." She sighed. "But for fifteen years I've followed the letter of the law. No speeding tickets. No parking tickets. I've kept my nose clean and avoided the police."

"I'm not the enemy."

"This isn't coming out right." She lifted her beer and finished off the rest of it before waving it in front of him. "I need another."

"Sure thing." He rose, sauntering over to the outdoor fridge. He pulled out two more, twisted off the tops, and set one in front of her before settling back down in his chair.

"Please understand why I moved around so much."

"Seriously, I get it. I do. You were afraid. I would be too." He tapped his finger on her knee. "The cop in me doesn't agree, but Emmerson, the man, totally understands."

"I can appreciate that. Thank you," she said. "Now, the text, because I'm not letting you off that easily."

He dropped his head to the table and groaned. "Why do you need to know?"

"Because I would bet this suitcase of cash that it has to do with me and if that's the case, I have a right to know what it said."

"You're not going to like it." He sat up taller. "And I'm not going to sugarcoat it for you either." He reached for his phone.

"What are you doing?"

"Asking my brothers to send me a copy of the text in question. That way you'll get the full picture of the insanity that is my family." He tapped away at his screen.

They waited for a minute or two in silence until his phone buzzed.

"Here you go. Read it for yourself. But fair warning, you might not ever look at my mother the same way again." He placed the cell on the table. "Or me for that matter."

She snatched it quickly before he changed his mind.

Rhett: *Not sure why you want this, but if you tell Mom I was the one who sent it you, I'll deny it. "If you two boys don't leave Mr. Saucy and Miss Saucy Pants alone right now,*

I'll come haul your asses out of there myself. That man needs to get laid. He's too fucking uptight to work with and she looks like she needs it as much as he does."

"Oh my fucking God." Rumor set the phone, screen down, on the table. "What kind of look was I giving her?"

"No idea, Miss Saucy Pants." He laughed.

"I don't think I like that nickname." She poked him in the arm. "But she's right about one thing."

"I'm terrified to ask what that is."

"You can be uptight."

He set his beer on the table and stood. He yanked her out of her chair and heaved her to his chest. "Well, I know one way to fix that."

Resting her hands on his shoulders, she stared into his dark, smoldering eyes. "Well, you have been ordered to be glued to my hip."

"That may be true, but I want it stated for the record." He reached down, curling his hands under her thighs and lifting her off the pool deck, wrapping her legs around his waist. "That I want to be with you and that has nothing to do with anything other than I really like you."

"Not to sour the mood or anything, but did you like me an hour ago?"

"Yes," he said. "I didn't like that you were withholding information, but I didn't believe for one second that you were involved. I just didn't understand why you couldn't trust me to tell me the truth.

Now I do." He kissed her softly. "Just please, no more secrets."

"That goes both ways." She arched a brow. "I want to know what's going on with this case. It concerns me and I don't want to be left in the dark."

"My mom won't tell us everything. Not even me. My job now is to make sure nothing happens to you, but what I know, you will know."

"Thank you."

"You're welcome," he said. "Anything else? Because I'm really uptight."

She laughed. "No. You can take me to bed now."

"Yes, Miss Saucy—"

She covered his mouth. "Don't say it. Not if you want to get laid."

"But it's true. You are saucy."

"You can say it if I can use the handcuffs." She winked.

"Never going to happen." He kissed her. Hard. It was filled with passion and intent. Maybe this was her safe harbor after all.

11

Reluctantly, Emmerson broke off the kiss and did his best to balance the woman in his arms while he snagged the suitcase of cash.

"What are you doing?" Rumor whispered, tickling his neck with her hot breath.

"I don't think it's a good idea to leave this out here, do you?"

"I guess not, but why don't you put me down."

"Not on your life," he said. "But I'll let you hold the handle. I mean, it is on wheels." He adjusted her body. She wasn't very heavy, but he wasn't as young as he used to be and he was still running on fumes. He managed to open the slider, clicking it locked behind him while she nibbled on his ear and neck, driving him crazy. He'd never met anyone like Rumor.

Gently, he laid her down on the bed, her legs still

tight around his waist. He stared into her soft, adoring eyes. Everything was happening so fast. His emotions were swirling around his gut like a race car at the track. He didn't know if he wanted to speed up or slow down.

He wasn't sure if he had any control at all anymore.

The only thing he did know for sure, was that Rumor had taken hold of his heart and he didn't think he'd ever get it back.

"What?" she whispered.

"You're beautiful."

"I'm already in your bed. You don't have to—"

He pressed his finger over her lips. "I'm saying it because I mean it. And also, I get the feeling you haven't heard it enough in your life."

A gasp echoed in the night as she sucked in a breath.

"Don't ever let anyone make you feel less than. Not even me. You're one special woman."

"Thank you." She palmed his cheek, running her thumb over his scruff. "This has to go."

"I know. I hate it. My five o'clock shadow starts at three, and by nightfall, it's out of control." He smiled. "But not until tomorrow, unless you tell me otherwise."

She gave him a good shove, rolling him to his back and straddling his hips. Ripping off her shirt, she reached behind her back and unclasped her bra, tossing it across the room.

His breath caught in his throat as he watched her, mesmerized by her confidence and beauty.

Their connection felt electric, every touch igniting a fire within them both. She traced the outline of his lips with her fingertips, teasing him with a mischievous smile. He couldn't help but be captivated by her, by the way she moved and the way she made him feel alive.

Her hair fell around them like a curtain, framing her face in an ethereal glow. His heart thudded loudly in his chest as she leaned down, pressing a trail of kisses along his jawline and neck.

She tugged at his shirt, yanking it over his head, and then dotted kisses across his stomach.

"What are you doing?" he asked.

"Removing the rest of your clothing." In an instant, his shorts were at his ankles.

"If I'm going to be naked, then you have to be too."

"All in good time." She curled her fingers around his length.

He hissed, dropping his head back on the pillow. His breaths came in short, choppy pants. He fisted the sheet and curled his toes, praying he didn't turn into a horny teenager as he stared down at the most erotic thing that had ever happened to him. "That's enough," he managed to croak out, tugging at her hair.

She stared at him, licking her lips.

"You're going to be the death of me." He slid off the edge of the bed, carefully removing her shorts and resting her legs over his shoulders. He kissed her intimately. Softly. Slowly at first. Savoring every lick. She tasted like honey and he wanted every last drop.

As he continued to explore her, she moaned softly, her hands gripping his hair, pulling him closer. Her breaths were ragged and he knew she was close to the edge.

Her sweet scent filled the room. She wriggled with every touch, rolling her hips with the motion of his tongue.

"Yes, Emmerson. Yes." Her climax slammed into his mouth.

He didn't need anything more. Her pleasure was all that mattered.

But once again, he found himself on his back, with her on top. She wasted no time guiding him inside, grinding her hips against him with wild abandon.

His hands tightened around her hips, pulling her against him, as she threw her head back in pleasure. He groaned, their bodies moving in perfect rhythm, the heat and friction between them building up to a crescendo.

She moaned his name, her eyes locked on his, and in that moment, their souls were intertwined.

Their eyes meeting was the only thing he needed—proof that this was more than just carnal desire. It was affection, it was—dare he even think it—love, and it was everything he'd ever dreamed of.

Their bodies shook with climax, their hearts pounding in unison as she fell to his chest, their breaths ragged and intermingled.

He held her close, running his hands up and down her back, unable to speak for fear he might actually utter the words *I love you*. It was too soon for that. Way too soon. And with danger lurking at every corner, he couldn't risk it. They would have time to discover more about each other. Time to fall in love properly.

He rolled to his side, tugging the covers over their bodies, taking a moment to reflect on his life. This was exactly the position he'd promised himself he'd never be in again. It wasn't about loving, but loving too quick. Trusting his heart to someone without holding a piece of it back.

Only, every other time he thought he'd been in love, that's what he'd done. He'd hidden parts of himself away. As if to keep them secret, only to be revealed when he deemed whoever worthy.

But that never happened.

He propped himself up on his elbow. "Is there anything you want to know about me?"

"That's an odd question right about now." She

traced her finger up and down his biceps. "What do mean?"

"I know a lot about your past. Do you have any burning questions about mine?"

"Have you done anything illegal?"

He burst out laughing.

"It's a legit question."

He cleared his throat. "There are levels of illegal and let's say I've committed a few misdemeanors in my day, but nothing that would land me in anything but county lockup for a night."

"I want details of the offenses and if you ever spent the night in jail."

"You're nuts," he said. "Okay. Let's see here. I ran naked through town."

"No way." She sat up, hugging the sheet to her chest. "How old were you?"

"Sixteen and my while my mom thought it was funny, she had to pretend she was pissed." He fluffed the pillow and adjusted himself a little taller. "I smoked pot in high school and while it's medically legally in this state now, it certainly wasn't back then. I jumped the fence to the state park after hours." He glanced toward the ceiling. "God, I'm lame and pretty much a Goody Two-shoes."

"You're a cop's kid. I think one would expect you to be."

He held up his index finger. "I did spend the night in the slammer when I was seventeen. But that was only because my mother made us all do that. She thought it would be a good lesson."

"That's just cruel."

"Nah. She put us in there when it was full of drunks and morons. It kind of did the trick," he said. "Anything else you want to know?"

"I kind of love this twenty questions thing." She tucked her hair behind her ears. "How old were you when you lost your virginity?"

"If I answer that, you have to as well."

"Deal." She nodded.

"Seventeen."

"Eighteen," she said. "With who? Where? And what was it like?" She tilted her head and batted her lashes.

"Really?"

"Oh yeah. I want to know the sordid details."

"You asked for it." No one he ever dated asked him questions like this, much less enjoyed the conversation. Not that he wanted to rehash his entire past, but this part of his life he could laugh at. It wasn't too serious, though slightly embarrassing. And it felt normal to share it with Rumor. "Her name was Stephanie and she was two years older than me."

"Interesting."

He chuckled. "My mother hated her, especially because she was older. But seventeen is legal consenting age, so Mother didn't have a leg to stand on and that burned her ass, especially when she found the box of condoms in my room. She went nuts, telling me that a woman like Stephanie was nothing but trouble."

"What did you do?"

"I was in my rebel against Mom stage, so I brought Stephanie around every chance I got."

Rumor shrugged against his body, resting her chin on his chest, and stared at him with wide eyes, hanging on his every word. She had a way of making him feel like he was the most important person in the room. It didn't matter that he was the only person around, because no one ever gave him this kind of attention.

Except his immediate family.

And they didn't count.

"To make a long story short, Stephanie was pretty experienced. She taught me a lot of things about sex."

"Like what, specifically?"

"I don't know. Like how to do it." He laughed. "Oral?"

"You mean that thing you did with your tongue?"

"Yeah. That." He shook his head. "We're getting sidetracked. The point is, she liked sex. A lot. Even my seventeen-year-old self struggled to keep up. One night, she got ahold of my mother's handcuffs."

"Oh my God." She lifted her head. "You let her tie you up."

"One of the biggest mistakes of my life." He let out a sigh. "I had a lot to learn about women and had no idea she was all that pissed at me for blowing her off to hang with my friends."

"Oh, that's not cool."

"It's not the worst, but yeah, I didn't even call her." He shrugged. "I thought she'd forgiven me. She hadn't. She cuffed me to bed. Naked. Mind you, this was at an abandoned camp. Left me there and then called the cops about a trespasser. Imagine my surprise when my mother walked in."

Rumor dropped her head to his chest and burst out laughing. "That has to be the funniest thing I've ever heard." She brushed her hair from her face. "Any chance I'll ever meet this girl?"

"Probably. She's married to a buddy of mine and lives in town."

"That's got to be awkward."

"Only when my mother brings up handcuffs." He arched a brow. "Your turn, only I'm guessing I don't want to hear about your first."

"No. That would just piss you off and sour the mood." She pressed her warm lips on his chest. "But I did once date this guy for a couple of weeks who had a foot fetish. He liked to suck my toes. It was gross and freaked me out. I had to break up with him."

"Yeah. I'll suck on a few things, but toes aren't one of them." He reached out, running his thumb over her bottom lip. "You're a strong woman. I can see that. But I'm sorry you've had to run for so long. I hate that you've never been able to settle in and see what life is like when you don't have to look over your shoulder. And that you've never been able to develop strong, lasting bonds with people." She opened her mouth, but he hushed her with his finger. "I get you've been doing it all on your own and I respect that. But you don't have to anymore. Not if you don't want to."

"Thank you for adding in that last part. It means a lot."

"I can be a real selfish prick when I want to be and I want you to give this community a chance. But I also know that your entire adult life has been built on moving. That's not an easy habit to break, even when you longer have to."

"Why are you saying this?"

Oh boy. He'd really gone and done it now. He might as well lay it on the line. "Because I care about you. Because I want to see where whatever this is between us can go." He kissed her softly. "I don't take many risks when it comes to matters of the heart. Both times I jumped in headfirst, I got burned. Since then, I've been dating here and there, but never really putting myself out there. Until you walked into my life. Now look at me. I'm a blubbering idiot."

"I would never call you that." She palmed his face. "But can we get through one thing at a time? Deal with the whole Tony and Tom thing before we define what we are or I go making any big plans to stay."

"I can live with that." His cell buzzed. He reached across her to the nightstand and lifted it, staring at a text from his father. "My dad will be here in ten minutes."

"Why?"

"He doesn't exactly say. Only says to get dressed and meet him at the door."

"How does he know you're not wearing clothes?"

"He doesn't, but he's making an educated guess based on a message from my mother." Emmerson waved his phone. "Shall I read you my dad's text?"

"Sure. Why not."

He laughed. "Hey. You and Rumor need to get out of bed, get dressed, and meet me at the door in ten. There's something we need to discuss. Something your mother didn't consider until after we spoke and it's important. Get moving, Saucy. Damn, that's an awful name. Who gave it to you anyway? See you shortly." He tossed back the covers, found his shorts, and hiked them up over his hips.

"If I had known that name was going to stick, I would have never said it."

"Trust me. They will tire of it. They always do."

"Are you sure about that?"

He nodded. "We used to call Miles Mr. Fingers. It lasted a month. And Jameson was Fireball for a while and after Stephanie, everyone called me Houdini, so yeah, it will disappear eventually."

"Good."

Ding-dong.

"My dad doesn't like to be kept waiting." He waved his finger over the bed.

She pulled the covers over her head. "I have no idea why I'm so utterly embarrassed."

"Of all the people in my family, he's the least likely to razz either one of us too hard. But everyone still acts like a bunch of stupid teenagers, so expect a little teasing." He leaned over, yanked the covers, and kissed her sweet lips. He'd never get enough of her. "Just remember it's more about me, than you. And they wouldn't do it if they didn't like you."

"Right."

"I'll see you out there." He snagged a shirt and made his way out of the bedroom and to the front door. "You could have used your key."

His father stepped into the foyer. He was starting to look his age with deep-set lines around his eyes and lips. His hair had begun to gray and thin and he'd put on a few pounds over the years, but he was still fit.

And handsome.

His dad was one of the fairest men Emmerson had ever known. Growing up, he'd always been the voice of reason, where his mom ruled with an iron gavel. Whenever any of the boys needed advice, they generally went to their dad, unless it was regarding police work. But even then, there were times Emmerson wanted his father's perspective. He could always see both sides of the coin, something his mother struggled with.

"You have a young woman in this house. I wasn't walking in on that." His dad slapped his shoulder. "I've only met her a couple of times, but she seems like a nice girl and your mother really likes her. Can't shut up about her. It's Rumor this. And Rumor that."

"Could have fooled me. One minute she was all over me to take her out. Next minute she was up my ass to stay away."

"It was all about the timeline, never the girl, but that's been cleared up."

"Do you want anything to drink? Eat?"

"I wouldn't say no to a beer." His dad eased onto one of the stools at the island, setting his briefcase on the counter. "I have to ask. Where did this Mr. Saucy shit come from? I feel so out of the loop."

"Believe it or not, Rumor started it." Emmerson pulled out two beers, setting one in front of his father. "It all started with a random comment about hand-cuffs." He waggled his finger. "At the time, she had no idea about Stephanie or what happened."

"And she does now?"

Emmerson ran his fingers through his hair. "Yeah."

"Wow. I'm shocked. You hate telling that story to anyone and we're not allowed to bring it up."

"I find myself willing to tell her all sorts of things." Emmerson leaned against the counter. "This thing with Rumor has come on hard and way too quick. I can't seem to slow it down and honestly, I'm not sure I want to and that's not like me." Emmerson often saved these types of conversations for Emmett. Or Rhett. They both shared some major heartbreak. So had Jameson. They commiserated with one another at different times in their lives. But now that they all had wives and were happy in their relationships, Emmerson found himself at a crossroads with his brothers. It wasn't that he couldn't confide in them.

He could.

But it was different.

And he didn't want to bring them down.

Besides, his father had always been a good sounding board and he understood Emmerson like no one else.

"Are you telling me this because you want my opinion? Or are you just saying it out loud to sort your thoughts."

"Perhaps a little of both."

His father took a slow sip of his beer. "You know I've always loved your mother and I always will."

"What does that have to do with my insane feelings for Rumor?"

"I couldn't let go of your mother because of you boys. And then there was Jameson. I made a commitment to raise him as my own. I can't regret that even though it hurt him." His dad raised his hand. "But your mom and I stopped loving each other the way a married couple should probably after Nathan was born. We kept having kids to keep our marriage together. Again, no regrets because you kids are everything to both of us. It bonded your mother and me in ways that are unbreakable and why we've been able to remain such good friends. But for me, it's made me like you in some ways."

"What does that mean?"

"Unable to trust." His father arched a brow. "You mom was in love with another man and that hurt. It took a long time for me to get over that and to be able to be with someone in a loving relationship and not stew in the past. To not sit and wait for the shoe to drop. I've watched the way you form relationships with women and it's always the same thing. You look for the flaws and the second you find one, you home in on it and expect the worst. But with Rumor, you knew she was hiding something and yet you trusted your gut instinct for the first time since Tessa."

"That was a mistake."

"Probably, but since then, you've never given anyone a chance." His dad lifted his beer. "And to be fair, you pushed Tessa away. The second you bought a house with her, you started walking out that door."

Emmerson stiffened his spine. "Are you trying to tell me it's my fault she cheated?"

"Not at all. She did that. But cheating isn't what ended that relationship. It was the straw that broke the camel's back." His dad tapped his finger on the counter. "Don't go looking for trouble where there isn't any. Rumor has baggage. She found herself in a shitty situation and she did a stupid thing out of fear. She had no support. No family. All she knew was abandonment, pain, loneliness, and the wrong side of the law. What's important is that she's doing what's right now and there's nothing wrong with falling hard and fast. Or for someone who has a checkered past. The key is communication and if you're telling her things, and she you, then you have nothing to worry about. It's when you stop talking that you need to be concerned."

"That's what happened to you and Mom? You stopped talking?"

"Your mother and I had seven boys to discuss. That's how we lasted as long as we did. But outside of that, she dedicated her life to this community and I worked long hours. We couldn't talk about what to have for breakfast without it being an argument." His dad tapped his temple. "Stop thinking so much. And if there is something that comes up and you need an answer, ask her the question. Don't sit around and wait for her, because all that will happen is you will end up closing yourself off from the best thing that's ever happened to you."

12

Rumor stared at herself in the mirror.

This is your safe harbor.

Could it really be the one place she could stay forever? Could she actually allow herself to bond with this town and the people in it? With Emmerson?

She'd spent her childhood living in fear and feeling alone. Her parents were never around, even before they had abandoned her. They were drug addicts, a fact she had to accept.

Foster care had been no walk in the park either.

She might as well have not even existed in most of the homes she'd lived in. While her adult life had been an adventure, she'd still been alone. She had no one to call family. No one to call in the middle of the night if she needed a friend.

Up until now, she told herself it didn't matter.

But it did.

She was thirty-three and she was tired of trying to tell herself she was happy.

She wanted a safe harbor.

A place to call home. Friendships. True bonds. Ones she could allow her heart to hold on to and have to say goodbye the moment her soul ached.

Squaring her shoulders, she stepped from the master bath and made her way through the house. She paused in the kitchen, listening to the deep voices. She couldn't make out what they were saying and she could barely tell which was Emmerson and which one his father. They were so similar. She picked up the picture on the table near the fireplace. It was taken at Rhett's wedding. The whole family. They were a good-looking bunch and it was obvious how much they loved and supported one another.

Her eyes burned as she gently set the frame back on the table. She'd brought them nothing but controversy and problems. She hated that for Emmerson and his family. They had done nothing but show her kindness, even Rebecca who had been harsh.

She'd only been doing her job.

Rumor couldn't blame her for that.

She inched closer to the kitchen, collecting her thoughts.

"Hey, you." Emmerson smiled. "You remember my dad."

"I sure do. Hi, Mr. Kirby."

"Please, call me Dalton." He rose, leaning in and kissing her cheek as if she belonged in this house. "I don't want to keep you two very long, so let me get right to the point." Dalton opened his briefcase and pulled out a piece of paper and a pen. "I used to be the district attorney, but two years ago, I left that position and became partners with my son Seth."

"That really burned my mother's ass." Emmerson laughed.

"Everyone deserves their day in court and what your mom fails to understand, we're not about seeing criminals get off, but about making sure—"

"Save the lecture, Dad. I got no beef with what you and Seth do." Emmerson pointed to the document on the counter. "What's that?"

"Rumor, do you have a few dollars you can give me?"

"Why am I doing that?" Rumor asked, glancing between Emmerson and Dalton.

"Because I need you to hire me as your attorney." He pushed the pen and paper across the table. "Sign that, hand me a few bucks as a retainer, and I'll get to the point."

"I don't like this." Rumor lifted the pen with a shaky hand. "Why do I need a lawyer?"

"I'm hoping that you won't ever need my services. But after Rebecca and I spoke about this situation, I pointed out something that could happen and we both agreed that there are a couple of scenarios that could lead to you needing me. But I can't get into them until you sign that. This way we will have attorney-client privilege. Make sense?"

"I guess so," she said softly, but she wasn't sure she followed.

Emmerson came up behind her and rested his strong hands on her shoulders, massaging gently. "It's okay. Do it." He reached around her and opened a drawer, pulling out a five-dollar bill. "Here you go, Dad."

"Perfect." Dalton placed the money and the document back in his briefcase. "Okay. Now, when Rebecca catches these assholes, and she will, we have no idea how it will play out."

"Yeah, we do. Those fuckers will go to prison for a very long time," Emmerson said.

"Well, there's that." Dalton held up his finger. "But there are some unknown factors we can't account for. We don't know if Tom is involved in Tony's plan to take down Rumor."

"I only met Tom a couple of times," Rumor said. "I wasn't involved in dealing drugs or anything. I wanted no part of that. I made that clear even though Tony didn't listen and kept trying to pull me in."

"This is part of the problem." Dalton folded his hands and rested them on top of his briefcase. "I called a few people I know out in California about that murder you witnessed. They know Tony did it, but they can't prove it. Since Tony went to prison, they consider it case closed. Two criminals off the streets. However, they want Tom. The heat got so bad for Tom that he moved his operation to Miami."

"Dad, get to the point," Emmerson said.

"Once Tom and Tony are arrested, it's possible they will do what most criminals in their situation will do and that's deflect, blame, and try to cut a deal. They will throw anyone under the bus. Now, they can't blame Rumor for anything that happened here in Lighthouse Cove. But that doesn't mean they don't have something else up their sleeve." He turned, pointing to the bag of cash sitting on the floor. "You took their drug money. You witnessed a murder. Whether you want to accept it or not, you have some knowledge of their operation back in California. And we have no idea how long they have been following you."

"Rhett and Miles already looked into where she's been and there has been no evidence of Tom's drugs or related crimes." Emmerson wrapped his arm around her and pulled her close, as if to protect her.

She loved him for that.

Love.

What a strong and strange concept. She'd never loved anyone in her life. The closest she'd ever come to it was George. But she hadn't loved him. She had deep feelings for him, which was why she boogied out of town. Getting too close to anyone was something she couldn't afford to do. Not only because it could put her in danger.

But them.

Emmerson represented everything she tried to avoid. Besides being a cop, he was the kind of man she had always dreamed of. He was caring. Honest where it counted. Tender and loving.

And he showed up when she needed him most.

Even George hadn't done that.

"I have them digging deeper, just to be prepared." His father arched a brow. "My point is Tony spent almost fifteen years in prison. Because of what Rumor did. If he told Tom, and Tom is giving him some leeway to get her back, who knows what they are doing to set her up. All this is worst-case shit. I don't think it will come to this. But I want our bases covered. That's why I had to come tonight. So that document was dated today. If anyone asks, I was here when you told your story to Rebecca. Tessa and Johnny have already agreed to that fact."

"Seriously? Tessa said she'd do that?" Emmerson asked. "I'm shocked. She hates me."

"That's not true." Rumor shifted her gaze. "If you believe that, you're a dumbass. She's hurt and I feel bad for what I said to her."

"I like this one. She's smart. And she's right. You and Tessa might not have been right for each other, but you're both holding on to displaced anger. Time to let that shit go," Dalton said, lifting his beer and taking another swig. "Rumor, if it comes down to them trying to pin anything on you, including that murder from fifteen years ago, we're going to have to sit down and have a serious conversation about exactly what happened. And you will have to make a formal statement. But let's hope it doesn't come to that." He stood. "I'll see myself out."

"Thanks, Dad. I appreciate the heavy dose of honesty."

"Call me if you need anything, son." Dalton gave Emmerson a man hug before taking her by the shoulders. "This family has adopted you as one of our own. We're not going to let anything happen to you." He kissed her cheek. "Make sure my boy here is taking good care of you. He can be a little moody at times, but he's a good egg."

"I agree on both counts." She wrapped her arms around Dalton. Never in her life had she felt so many emotions in one day. But mostly, she felt safe. "Thank you."

"Anytime, darling." Dalton snagged his briefcase and waved his free hand over his head.

"You look almost exactly like your father," Rumor whispered.

"I get that a lot." He kissed her forehead. "For the record, I'm not moody."

She laughed. "Yes, you are. But I would be too if I had your job. Honestly, I don't know how you do it."

He lifted her off the ground and set her ass on the

counter, wrapping her legs around his waist. "I've told you before, being a cop in this small town is mostly boring. I scare kids out of the park at night. I deal with stolen bikes. Give speeding tickets. Sometimes the most excitement I have is dealing with naked neighbors having sex in open spaces." He arched a brow.

"Seriously?"

"A few months ago, we got a call about a couple who were constantly doing the nasty in their outside shower for all the neighbors to see. The problem in this state is if you have a cage over your pool, it's kind of considered inside and if you want to walk around naked, you can. But they didn't have a cage. We had to ask them to stop. Only, when I got there, they were in the middle of it."

"Live porn. What fun."

"Not really. They were seventy-eight. It was almost worse than walking in on your mother and her new husband."

"Oh God. That had to have been embarrassing… for your mom." Rumor rested her hands on his shoulders. Her chest tightened and her heart fluttered. No way could she be falling in love with this man. It couldn't happen this quick.

And certainly not to her.

"All I can say about that is thankfully I didn't actually see anything because it would have scarred me worse than having my mother see me naked, handcuffed to a bed." He closed his eyes and shook his head. "With my brother standing there laughing his ass off."

"Oh my. You didn't tell me that juicy piece of information before." She palmed his cheek.

He blinked.

"The five o'clock shadow is sexy, but once it gets to this, you start looking like a bum."

"I know. The only one of us boys who can do facial hair is Rhett. But he is a bum," Emmerson said with a beaming smile. "I'll shave it in the morning. Right now, I have other things on my mind." He tugged her shirt over her head and pinched her nipple with his thumb and forefinger.

She groaned, dropping her head back, threading her fingers through his short hair as he sucked her nipple into his mouth. She couldn't get enough of him and she never wanted it to end. She'd sailed into this town and it had touched her heart.

But Emmerson had stolen it and her soul.

He dotted kisses down her stomach as he removed her shorts and panties, tossing them haphazardly to the side. He licked the inside of her thigh, staring up at her with an adoring gaze.

It nearly brought tears to her eyes.

He ran his finger over her hard nub, teasing and toying with her until she begged him to give her the satisfaction only he could deliver. He smiled before diving two fingers inside and lapping at her clit with her legs draped over his shoulders.

She gripped the sides of the counter. Her breaths came in short, raspy pants while she watched him please her until she cried out his name, trembling in the purest of delight.

Never had she felt so loved. Valued. Appreciated. Sexy. A gamut of conflicting emotions washed over her body.

She loved him.

A fact she could no longer deny.

It was the single most gratifying sensation she'd ever felt. And yet she resented it. She resented him for making her fall in love.

She believed he cared, because Emmerson wasn't the kind of man to take a woman to bed if he didn't. But after everything he'd been through, she knew he'd never be able to fully give another girl his entire heart again. It wasn't so much because he was broken, even though he was, a little. But because he was so guarded, he could never truly let anyone in.

Not even her.

Not even now.

And she felt his reserve.

He pulled her from the counter and quickly shed his clothes. He stared at her with hunger in his gaze. He turned her, spreading her legs, bending her slightly over the counter.

She gasped as he thrust himself inside her with a

quick jerk, holding on to her hips. His movements were desperate.

Wild.

And out of control.

He groaned, spilling his climax into her as he kissed her shoulder and neck, whispering her name over and over again. It sounded so sweet. So caring.

His hands ran up and down her arms and back with a gentle touch, as if they hadn't just defamed his kitchen counter. As if the sex hadn't been… well, just hot and heavy sex.

The way he behaved, it was more like they had just made love.

As if there was a distinction.

"I don't know about you," he whispered in her ear. "But I will never be able to eat breakfast again and not think about this." He nibbled on her ear. "Or you ever again."

"Why, Emmerson, that has to be the sweetest thing you ever said." She turned, wrapping her arms around his thick body, hugging him tight, trying not to think about the fact she was completely naked in his kitchen. Or that the air was thick with sex.

He chuckled. "Come on. Let's go to bed." He took her by the hand and walked gloriously naked through the house, taking only his cell with him.

Snuggling beside him, she rested her head on his chest and stared out the sliders at the pool.

"Can I ask you a stupid question?" he said softly. His fingers danced up and down her arm.

"Sure. But if it's really dumb, I might not answer."

"I love your sense of humor. Actually, I love everything about you."

Love. He didn't mean it the same way she felt it.

"Does our age difference bother you?" he asked.

She lifted her head, catching his gaze. "That's an odd question. Does it bother you?" She swallowed. Hard. Her brain scrambled to find a hidden meaning to the conversation.

"I asked first." He batted her nose. Why did he have to be so playful all the time?

"It's what, nine, ten years?"

"It's almost ten," he said. "So when I was having sex for the first time, you were seven."

"That's a dumb way of looking at things and no, your age doesn't bother me. If it did, I wouldn't be in this bed with you. Your turn to answer."

"I'll be honest, it did at first. But it doesn't now." He lifted her chin and kissed her so softly and tenderly, she wanted to cry. "Good night, Rumor."

"Sleep well, Emmerson." She let out a long breath and settled in for the night.

She had no idea what the future held. But she did know one thing. She belonged to him and she couldn't fight it, even though deep down she knew this couldn't last. Even if she could stay in Lighthouse Cove when all of this was over, she wasn't sure she would be able to. She knew nothing of putting down roots. It didn't matter that she wanted to. Or that she was falling for Emmerson. She knew his history. He'd been honest about his past with women and trust didn't come naturally.

Loving someone wouldn't come easy to Emmerson, a fact she couldn't deny.

His concern about her age proved it. He was already looking for the holes. For reasons why this wouldn't work. She didn't need to know him long to know that about him.

And then there was her wandering soul, as he put it.

This is your safe harbor.

God, she so desperately needed one. She needed him. Wanted him and everything he represented.

In that moment, she made the decision she would stay until he decided it was over and someday it would be over. Someday he would walk away because Emmerson couldn't give his heart.

13

Emmerson bolted upright and reached for his phone.

"What is that noise?" Rumor sat up and rubbed her eyes.

"It's the alarm to the pool house." Emmerson jumped from the bed, found a pair of jeans, and hiked them up over his hips. He retrieved his weapon and clip, slamming it into position. His heart thumped in his chest.

"What does that mean?"

"It means someone just broke in," he said. "Hey Siri, call The Boss." He raced to the sliders and peered out the window, but none of the lights were on. Fuck. Someone must have shut them off. But how? The breaker was in the garage. That alarm should have gone off first and he knew he engaged it.

Or had he.

Shit. He hadn't. Not after his father left.

Damn it.

"Emmerson. It's fucking four in the morning. This better be—"

"Ma, I've got an intruder. I forgot to turn on the house alarm last night after Dad left. The only one that was on was the pool house and it just went off."

"Shit. All right. Chris is on patrol tonight. I'll call Emmett. He's the closest and can be there in ten. I'll be there shortly after."

"Tell Chris not to come in with lights on. I'll see you soon." He ended the call, tucking his cell in his back pocket, and turned.

Rumor clutched the sheets to her chin and stared at him with wide, fearful eyes. He didn't have time to comfort her, even though all he wanted to do was take her in his arms, hold her, and tell her how much he cared.

And that it would be okay.

"Put some clothes on and stay right here until I get back," he said in a stern voice.

"You can't leave me here. Besides, my clothes are in the kitchen. I've got nothing to change into."

He raced to his dresser and pulled out a pair of boxers and a T-shirt. "Put these on." He tossed them at her.

Crash!

He jerked as the sound of breaking glass filled the air.

"Fuck."

"What was that?" Rumor tumbled out of the bed, crash-landing on the floor.

He raced to her side, helping her to her feet and tugging the shirt over her head.

She hobbled into the boxers.

"Stay right behind me, got it?"

"What the hell is going on?" She gripped his arms.

"I don't know. But I need you to do exactly what I say." He turned, holding his weapon at the ready. "I'm sorry if I'm being harsh or acting like a dick, but I take it personally when someone invades my space." He took out his phone and quickly sent a text to Emmett, his mom, and Chris with an update. It was just a few words.

Intruder broke into main house.

"I'm not upset by how you're acting," she whispered. "I'm just scared shitless."

So was he, but he wasn't about to tell her that.

Slowly, he tugged open the bedroom door and inched out into the pitch-black hallway. He let his eyes adjust to the darkness. It wasn't the first time he'd been in a dangerous situation. Hell, he was a cop. He'd been shot at before. Even took a bullet once.

But never in his life had anyone dared invade his home.

He rounded the corner into the family room. The sliding glass doors to the patio had been shattered.

"Watch your feet," he whispered as he maneuvered around the sofa.

A shadow to his left caught his attention. He jerked his body, keeping Rumor tucked behind him, but another shadow slinked out from the kitchen to his right and he froze as he stared at the wrong end of a gun.

"I'd put that down if I were you," Tony said as he flicked on the lights that hung over the island.

"I will do no such thing." Emmerson sucked in a deep breath, aiming his weapon dead center at Tony's chest.

Rumor dug her nails into Emmerson's back. She gasped as the other shadow emerged.

Tom.

Fucker.

Two guns.

Pointed at Emmerson.

And Rumor.

This was not good.

"You're going to hand over your gun and give us the girl. Otherwise, we start shooting," Tom said, waving his weapon like a fucking lunatic. He stood approximately six-two and was an impressive man, to say the least. Muscular. Fit. Surprisingly so for a man known for snorting his own product. His biceps bulged and were lined with tattoos. His hair was pulled back in a ponytail. And his face looked like leather from too much sun.

Tony, on the other hand, was a scrawny fellow. Not much meat on his bones and Emmerson knew without a doubt he could take that kid. But at what cost? He couldn't disarm both men at once. Not without one of them shooting and by the look in Tony's eye, he was higher than a fucking kite.

Bad sign.

"You can have my gun. You can even have me. But you're not taking Rumor anywhere." Emmerson released his grip on his gun and held his hands up. These two assholes had no idea the cavalry had been called. All Emmerson had to do was buy some time. His life—and Rumor's—was in the hands of his family and Chris. He trusted them and had faith that if he could contain the situation long enough, they would save the day.

They always did.

Tom snatched the gun from his fingertips. "We're not fucking around. That woman stole from us. And then she sent my boy up the river. If you think we're going to let her get away with that, you've got another thing coming."

"Well, you boys have a different problem because I don't believe you know who I am." Emmerson reached behind his back, holding Rumor tight to his body. His job was to protect her and he'd do that, or die trying.

Not because his mother told him to, but because his heart commanded it.

He loved her. No denying it and he wasn't even going to try.

"We know you're a cop," Tom said. "And we don't care. Home invasions happen all the time." Tom grabbed Rumor by the hair and yanked her from Emmerson's grasp.

She screamed.

He clenched his fists at his sides. A sense of dread and hopelessness filled his soul. "You're not going to get away with this."

"Take care of this asshole." Tom waved his gun toward Tony.

"You want me to kill the cop?" Tony's voice screeched and he lowered his gun slightly. "You said you'd handle it. That I'd get to deal with her."

"Oh, I'll let you have all your fun with this one in due time. But first, you have to handle him." Tom smiled. "It's how you prove your loyalty to me after trying to fuck me over in the first place."

Emmerson had no idea how far out his family was and he couldn't wait. He had to take matters into his own hands or surely, he and Rumor would die.

And he didn't feel like dying today.

Tony raised his gun a little higher with a shaky hand.

Emmerson lunged forward, diving toward Tom and Rumor.

Bang!

The bullet tore through his shoulder, jerking his

body as he tackled Tom and Rumor, dropping them both to the floor. The pain seared straight to his brain, but he did his best to ignore it as he reached for his weapon that went skidding across the tile.

He curled his fingers around the butt of the weapon as Tom hurled his body on top of Emmerson's.

Rumor screamed again, but he couldn't even glance up to see what that was about as Tom landed his fist right in Emmerson's nose. That fucking hurt almost as bad as the hole in his shoulder.

Bang!

He continued to fight with Tom until he got the upper hand, sticking his gun into Tom's side. "Don't make me pull the trigger."

Tom struggled to break free, kicking and swinging his arms, reaching for his weapon. The second his fingers touched the gun, Emmerson knew he had no choice. He had to fire.

Bang!

Tom's body went limp.

Emmerson shoved him to the side.

The sound of boots crushing broken glass filled the thick air.

"Run and I'll shoot you," Emmett's voice echoed in the night. "Fuck. I warned you."

Bang!

Emmerson jumped to his feet.

Chris and his mother barreled through the front door.

Emmett reached down and pressed his finger against Tony's neck. He shook his head. "He's gone. He didn't leave me a choice."

"Neither did Tom." Quickly, Emmerson checked for a pulse.

Nothing.

He turned his head.

Rumor lay on her side, curled in a ball, holding her stomach as blood flowed through her fingers.

"Rumor!" Emmerson dropped to his knees at her side, pressing his hands against the wound.

She blinked.

"Ambulance is ten minutes out." His mother rested a hand on his shoulder. "We need to stop your bleeding too."

"I'm fine." He jerked her hand off his shoulder, examining Rumor's wound more closely. "The bullet didn't go through," he said softly. "Stay with me, babe. It's going to be okay." Only, he wasn't so sure. Blood oozed from her gut. So much blood and her face paled.

Her chest rose and fell in a shallow breath.

His mom sat on the floor, cradling Rumor's head in her lap, stroking her hair. "Keep pressure on that wound." She waved her hand to Chris. "Get something to make a tourniquet for Emmerson."

"Ma. I told you, I'm fine. We need to—"

"Shut up, son. That bullet went right through and you're losing a lot of blood too. You won't be any good to her if you pass out. Let Chris at least tie it off."

Arguing with his mother wouldn't be helpful, so he let Chris do what she demanded while he pushed on Rumor's midsection.

She moaned and her eyes slowly closed.

"Come on, babe. Open your eyes," he said. "I'm not going to lose you now. I won't have it."

"I'm sorry to have brought this to you," she whispered.

"You have nothing to be sorry about. I'm the one who should be apologizing." He leaned over and kissed her sweet lips. "Now, I need you to fight. You hear me. You have too much to live for. We have too much to look forward to."

Jameson raced through the front door, followed by the paramedics, who tried to shove him out of the way, but he wouldn't budge.

"Emmerson." Jameson placed a hand on his shoulder. "You need to get out of their way and let them do their job."

Emmerson nodded as two more first responders came in. He stood, taking a step back, and watched in horror as they began to hook her up to an IV and lift her onto a gurney.

"Sir, we need to get you to the hospital too," one of the paramedics said.

"I want to go with her." He pointed to Rumor.

"She's in good hands." Jameson stepped in front of him. "You're going to the same place and not only do you need some serious stitches, but we have no idea what kind of damage that bullet did internally. I'll ride with you, now let's go. The faster we get there, the faster we'll know what's going on with Rumor."

Emmerson ran a hand over his unshaven face. He'd promised her he would shave and he'd be damned if the next time she saw him it would be with this scruff on his face. He glanced at his mother.

"Chris, Emmett, and I will handle everything here," his mom said. "Go."

He wiped the tear that had escaped his eye. "Ma, if they weren't already dead, I'd kill them."

"I know," she said.

He swallowed his beating heart. "I love Rumor."

"I know that too. Now get out of here. Get that shoulder taken care of. She's going to need you."

Following Jameson out the front door, he climbed into the back of the ambulance. The other one was already racing through the neighborhood. He sat down, leaned back, and closed his eyes. "She has to be okay. It can't end this way."

Emmerson held Rumor's hand, rubbing his thumb over the back side. Machines beeped in the background. An IV drip pumped medication and fluids into her system.

The sounds of people shuffling their feet in the hallway were a distant murmur.

"Hey, son." His mother strolled into the room and set a coffee and something that smelled like bacon and a fried egg on the table next to Rumor's bed. "Did you sleep here all night?"

"I'm not sure I'd call it sleep, but yeah."

"I figured you might." She pointed to the bag. "You need to eat if you're going to heal."

"I will." He lifted the coffee to his lips and sipped. "Any word on the other men helping Tom and Tony?"

"Picked up a few hours ago and I was there when

State took their statements. All part of setting her up to take the fall for the murders. They wanted her to pay for sending Tony to prison, but they picked the wrong town to do it in," his mom said. "Has she woken up?"

He shook his head. It had been touch and go for a while. They had to stabilize her before operating, and then it was a six-hour surgery to remove the bullet and repair the damage. Thank God no internal organs had been hit. She'd been lucky. "The doctors can't give me a reason why she hasn't come to and they said they wouldn't really try anything until this morning. Something about her body needing rest."

"They're right." She squeezed his good shoulder. The other arm was completely useless. While the bullet had gone in and out clean and all he needed was a good flush and stitches, he was in a sling for three weeks. Then physical therapy. It would be two months before he was back in business. "How are you feeling?"

"Like shit," he admitted.

"At least they didn't hit your shooting arm or writing hand."

He glared.

"What?" His mother shrugged. "After you take some time off to help Rumor recover, you're going to be on desk duty pushing papers."

"What if she doesn't wake up?" That thought had been weighing on his brain for hours. He'd been talking to her, telling her of all the dates he planned on taking her on. Long walks on the beach. Boat rides. Romantic dinners. He told her stories about his past. His childhood. Things he was afraid of. Things he never told anyone. Anything he could think of that might get her to peek open even a single eye.

But he got nothing.

"Don't talk like that," his mom said. "She needs you to be strong and she's going to need a lot of help for the first couple of weeks. You need to be her rock."

"Yes, ma'am."

"Jameson, Rhett, and Miles are at your place now. It's cleaned up. You can't tell anything happened."

"Except I've got no sliders," he mumbled.

"Jameson called in a few favors and found your doors. They are installing them as we speak. It will take a couple of days, but the doors will be fixed before you take her home."

Home.

God, how he wanted to make a home with Rumor. He wanted to jump into the deep end, but he didn't want to scare her away.

"Now, eat that damn breakfast sandwich I brought you. I have to go to the station. I'll be back as soon as I can."

He rubbed his clean-shaven face. After he'd been taken care of and while she was in surgery, his family forced him to go home and take a shower. His stomach growled. He dug his hand into the bag and pulled out the food. Lucy Ann made the best bacon, egg, and bagel sandwiches he'd ever tasted. Better than his own.

His mother hovered, waiting for him to dig in.

He took a big bite and his taste buds went wild, while his guilt ate him alive. If only he'd been able to buy a little more time, Rumor wouldn't have been shot. Maybe if he'd stayed in the bedroom a few minutes longer.

Fuck. He could do this to himself all day, but it wouldn't change a damn thing.

"I love you, Emmerson." His mom leaned over and kissed his temple like she'd done a thousand times when he'd been a small boy. "Call me when she wakes up."

"I will. I promise." He leaned back in his chair and finished his sandwich. He took a few more big gulps of his coffee, letting the caffeine hit his brain before taking her hand again and giving it a good squeeze. "Come on, babe. All your vitals are strong. Pulse is solid. Blood pressure is normal. You're breathing on your own. You don't even need oxygen, so please, open your eyes for me, Rumor."

Her finger twitched.

His heart went into overdrive. He stood, leaning closer, pressing his mouth over her dry lips. "That's it, honey. Wake up."

A tiny moan escaped her lips. Her eyes blinked. A

groan. Then a gasp and her eyes opened wide. "Emmerson?"

"I'm right here, sweetheart."

"Where am I?" She turned her head left, then right. Fear filled her beautiful eyes. "What happened? Where's Tony? Tom?"

"Shhhh, babe. They can't hurt you anymore." He ran his hand over her forehead and down the side of her face. "You're in the hospital and you're safe."

She tried to shift and winced in pain.

"Try not to move," he whispered. "You were shot. The doctors had to remove the bullet. You're going to be sore for a bit."

"That's not sore. That fucking hurts."

He chuckled. "That's the Rumor I know."

She reached out and tentatively touched his arm in the sling. "I remember seeing you get shot. All that blood spewing from your body. I thought for sure they had killed you."

"Nothing but a flesh wound. I'll heal up nice and quick. Nothing for you to worry your pretty little head about." He reached for the call button and pressed it.

"What are you doing?"

"The doctors are going to want to know you're awake." Carefully, he sat on the edge of the bed. "You gave everyone quite the scare. You've been asleep since your surgery and that was yesterday."

She palmed his face. "You shaved."

"I didn't want you to see me looking like a bum."

She cracked a half smile, but it quickly went away. "I remember lots of gunfire. What happened to Tony and Tom?"

"They're both dead."

She inhaled sharply. "Am I a bad person for not feeling horrible about that?"

"While I take no pleasure in ending anyone's life, including theirs, they were going to kill us. So, no, you're not a bad person. Far from it." He traced her jawline. "Are you thirsty? I don't know if you're allowed to eat, but I do know you can have some water."

"I am thirsty."

He snagged the cup of water with the straw the nurses had left. "Here you go." He held it to her mouth. His pulse had finally started to calm.

She was alive.

And awake.

Now all he had to do was convince her to stay.

"You called… oh. The patient is awake." The morning nurse, a woman by the name of Janet, strolled to the side of the bed. "How are you feeling?" Janet touched Rumor's arm.

"Like I was shot in the gut."

"A sense of humor is always a good sign." Janet nodded. "I'll let the doctor know and he'll want to come in and examine you."

"How long am I going to have to stay here?" Rumor asked.

"Already itching to get out. Another good sign. Only the doctor can answer that, but I would gather at least a few more days." Janet patted Rumor's arm. "He'll be in shortly."

"Thank you, Janet," Emmerson said.

"Anything for you and your family." Janet smiled. "Especially after what you did for me a few years ago." She waggled her finger. "And don't go popping those stitches. I don't want to see you back in my ER like when you were shot in the thigh."

"No, ma'am."

Janet marched her ass out of the room.

"You've been shot before? And you're on a first-name basis with my nurse, Mr. Saucy."

He laughed. It felt so good to laugh. "For the record, I've known Janet my entire life. We graduated high school together."

"Have you dated her too?"

"Why, Rumor, are you jealous?"

"No. Curious is more like it."

"She actually went to Emmett's senior formal. So, me dating her would have been weird, especially because I think they had sex."

"Think or know?" she asked, reaching for the water.

"He's never confessed and neither has she." Emmerson took a napkin and wiped the few drops of water that dribbled down her chin.

"So, tell me, how did you get shot in the thigh?"

Everything was so easy with Rumor. Here she was, lying in a hospital bed after major surgery, sleeping for hours, and she was chatting away like it was nothing.

He loved that about her.

He loved everything about her.

But this wasn't the right moment to tell her.

It had to be perfect.

"I got called to a domestic disturbance call about eight years ago. It happened to be Janet. I got between her and her ex-husband and he shot me."

"You took a bullet for another woman?"

"Oh my, someone is jealous." He batted her nose.

"No. I'm just wondering if this is a thing."

"I try not to, but my job is to protect and serve. It's a hazard of the job, which is mostly boring and I'm hoping to never get shot at again. Or have to see my girlfriend crumpled on the floor with a gunshot wound to her abdomen. I can't say that I liked that very much." He ran his thumb over her lower lip. "I'm so sorry I couldn't prevent that from happening. I tried. I really did. If I could have taken that bullet, I would have."

A tear rolled down her cheek.

He wiped it away.

"You did everything you could to save us both." She cleared her throat. "I want to go back to this girlfriend thing you managed to slip in."

"Ah. That," he said. "I thought it was a given. Have I misread something?"

"As long as you keep shaving, I'll consider you my boyfriend."

"I'll do it twice a day if that's what it takes." Maybe it was the right time. But before he could get the words out, the doctor pulled back the curtain.

It would have to wait.

Rumor took Emmerson's hand as he helped her from the front seat of his personal SUV.

"You okay?"

"Hurts like a motherfucker. But I'm fine."

He chuckled. "Come on. Let's get you in bed and I'll make you some eggs." He guided her toward the main house.

"I live in the pool house." She arched a brow.

"Not while you're recovering, you don't." He opened the front door. "There is no way you could get in and out of that Murphy bed. Besides, I still have another eight days off work. I'm going to be your nurse for that time."

"I don't want you hovering. I can…" She groaned. "…take care of myself."

"Not yet, you can't."

She paused in the center of the family room and glanced around. Her body shook involuntarily as her mind relived the horrors of what happened.

Emmerson wrapped his loving arms around her, gently tugging her to his chest. "If staying here is too much, I can ask my mom if we can stay with her and Steve. We'd have an entire wing to ourselves."

"No." She shook her head. "I've put your family out enough." During the five days she'd been awake in the hospital, each and every one of his family members had come to visit. They all brought flowers and homemade food for her to enjoy.

Along with fun conversation.

The best news had been Trinity and Emmett had become parents. They adopted a little baby girl.

They named her Leslie Rumor Kirby because she had been born almost exactly at the time of the shooting. Poor Emmett had missed the birth, but Trinity had been there.

Rumor still didn't understand why they used her name, but she didn't dare question.

"Babe, you're not putting anyone out. I care about you and so does my family. We're all here for you."

She'd been listening to Emmerson say those words for days. She knew he cared. There wasn't even a doubt in her mind about that.

But how long would it last?

How long could she continue to live in his pool house, loving him as much as she did, knowing she'd never have all of him? He gave her as much as he could.

But he'd never utter those words.

"I don't know what I'd do without you," she whispered, knowing she shouldn't hint at anything.

"Lucky for you that you don't have to find out." He pressed his hand on the small of her back. "I took the liberty of gathering most of your things and putting them in my bedroom. I can stay in there with you, but if it hurts for me to be in bed with you, I can sleep down the hall."

"I don't think I can handle being alone," she admitted.

Not one single night did Emmerson leave her alone. He'd sneak out in the morning, go home, shower and shave, only to return and stay all day. Janet, nurse, would make up the recliner with sheets and a blanket, and he'd sleep there, even though Rumor told him he didn't have to.

He cared.

It felt like love, but what did she know? She thought her parents had loved her, but they abandoned her the first chance they got.

He pulled back the covers and fluffed the pillows, helping her ease in, while he sat on the edge, holding her hands. He sported a contemplative look, which made his forehead crinkle. He always did that when he had something serious he wanted to talk about but didn't know how to start.

"What's wrong?" She decided to help him along. Whatever they were going to be to each other, she wanted it to be good. However it ended, she wanted to cherish the moments.

"You know how Rhett and Miles were doing some deeper digging into your background and where you lived when we were dealing with the whole Tom and Tony thing?"

"Yeah."

"Well, they found your parents." He lifted his gaze. "I'm sorry I didn't tell you sooner. I've only been sitting on it for three days. But I wanted you to be physically stronger. Please don't be mad. I hate it when you're angry with me."

She stared at him with her heart thumping wildly in her chest. "My parents," she whispered. "Where are they? What happened to them? Have they been looking for me?"

"God, this breaks my heart," he said softly. "I don't have a lot of details and we have no idea why they left you and didn't come back. But when you were about sixteen, your father was arrested."

"For what?"

Emmerson closed his eyes for a long moment before blinking them open. "Your mother had died of an overdose and he did nothing to prevent it. He went to prison for manslaughter and took his own life shortly after. Babe, I'm so sorry. I wish I had better news."

"At least I know." Tears poured out of her eyes. She couldn't stop them if she tried. They weren't tears of sorrow. Or of great regret. They were just tears of sadness for the years of wondering. "My folks often left me for periods of time while they went on benders. They could have come back and found me gone and just kept going because I'm not sure they ever wanted me anyway. I've been used to that my entire life. To most of my foster care families, I was a meal ticket."

"Oh, sweetheart." He cupped her face. "You're wanted right here. With me. My family. You're part of us and this community. Don't you ever forget that." He kissed her tenderly and with intent. It was beautiful and for the first time in her life, she felt as though she belonged.

As if she had a home.

As if she had something and someone to hold.

But two things needed to be cleared up if she was going to stay. One might put her back in the pool house. But she needed to say it.

However, she'd deal with the other situation first.

"Emmerson, I need to talk to you about something."

"What is it?"

She pointed to the bag of money taunting her from the open closet. She found it funny that the master had his and hers and the hers was empty as shit, except the few things he'd hung in there that belonged to her. "I know your mom said I could keep it. And I actually need that money. I have five thousand in the bank that is mine. But I have been dipping into that here and there. Now, it seems so dirty. Like it's blood money and it makes me sick just to think about it."

"I can't say I like having it in my house. However, I've learned over the years not to argue with my mom about certain things. That would be one of them." He arched a brow. "What would you do with it if you didn't keep it?"

"Donate it to a women's shelter? Or maybe a drug rehab program," she said. "Only problem is if I do that, I'm so strapped for cash, renting your—"

He hushed her with his index finger. "I'm not taking rent from my girlfriend. That feels so icky. And before you go arguing with me, I had decided that while you were asleep in the hospital." He cocked his head. "You can do whatever you want with that bag of loot and I'm happy to help you donate it to a good cause. I'd love to do that, and I'm happy to help you save up some money."

"But you can't let me live here—"

"I'm not going to flex my muscles often, but this is

not negotiable. You're my girlfriend. I'm not taking your money."

"I'm not moving in with you." Even if he did say the words back, it was too soon. Even she understood that.

"I'm not asking you to, but for the next few weeks, you're not getting out of this bed," he said. "Now, how about I go make us some breakfast because I'm starving." He batted her nose and stood.

"Okay." Telling him how she felt would have to wait.

Emmerson dumped the scrambled eggs onto two separate plates, along with bacon, sausage links, and home fries. He wasn't the best cook, but he could cook the shit out of breakfast. He snagged the mugs of coffee and put everything on a tray.

He glanced up and scowled. "What the hell are you doing out of bed?"

Rumor held one hand over her midriff and used the other to grip the table and then the sofa as she made her way toward the kitchen. "I'm tired of being on my back."

Racing to her side, he put her arm around his good shoulder. The other one still hurt like hell, but he was a fast healer and had already started stretching it here and there, even though the doctor had told him to take it easy.

Hell, he didn't know the meaning of the word, unless a fishing reel was in his hand.

"Why is your arm out of your sling?" she asked.

"Easier to make breakfast." He tried turning her back toward the bedroom, but she protested.

"I want to eat like a normal person. At the table. Or maybe outside and get a little fresh air."

"That's against my better judgment."

"Yeah, well, it's not negotiable." She tilted her head, glaring.

"Fine." If only he could lift her into his arms.

Once he got her settled, he brought the food out and set it up, settling in next to the woman who rocked his world. One of these days he'd get the courage to tell her how he really felt. He showed her every day, but he knew that wasn't enough. She needed to hear him say the words.

She pushed her food around the plate.

"Why aren't you eating?"

She dropped her fork and let out the longest breath ever. "I can't do this a second longer." She lifted her gaze. "I have to know how you really feel about me. Not knowing is slowly killing me inside. I understand if you don't feel the same way. I get it. You have deep wounds. I do too."

He opened his mouth to interrupt her, but she talked so fast he couldn't get in a single word.

"I've never had these feelings before. I've never allowed it. I've never stayed in one place long enough for it to happen and besides, I've been too afraid of it. I keep trying to say the words, but I'm utterly terrified that if I do, I'll be banished to the pool house. Which eventually I'll have to go back there, because even if you do feel the same way I do, we're not ready for the living together shit. You act like a man who is… is… in… Jesus, I can't even get there because I don't even know what this looks like. I'm a grown-ass woman. I've been taking care of myself my entire adult life, but I don't know shit about this one thing." She dropped her hands in her lap and lowered her head. "I don't even know how to say it."

Emmerson pushed his plate across the table and turned his chair while he processed every single word that had come out of her mouth. He totally understood her trepidation. He had the same problem. He'd been holding back as much as she had, only he had no idea that's what she'd been doing.

They'd both been through a lot in the last few weeks.

And she'd been running and hiding her entire life, never really knowing what true love was all about.

At least he knew what that looked like. He'd felt it. He'd had loving relationships, even if they'd turned to shit.

He shifted her chair and lifted her chin with his

thumb and forefinger. "Let me get us both there. Say it for both of us."

"I'm not even sure I made sense." She kept her gaze anywhere but connecting with his.

"Look at me."

She blinked.

"I haven't made this easy for you. I'm moody and I've been hurt, leading you to believe that it's impossible for me to love again. To completely give of myself. Before I met you, I thought that was true. I've wanted to tell you how I feel, but honestly, I've been afraid."

"Of what?" More tears.

God, he hated making her cry. That was the last thing he wanted to do. She'd had enough of that in her life.

"That I'd scare you so badly you'd pack your bags and move in the middle of the night. I thought if I told you that I love you, it would—"

"You what now?" She grabbed his face. "I'm honestly not sure I heard that correctly. And to be fair, no one has ever said those words to me and meant them."

"Aw, now that just breaks my heart," he said. "I love you, Rumor. And I mean it from the bottom of my heart."

"How I wish we could get saucy between the sheets, because I love you right back."

"Yeah, it's going to be a few weeks before we can

defile anything else in this house." He jerked his finger over his shoulder toward the dock. "Or my boat, because it hasn't been christened yet."

"I could be down for some ocean sex." She swiped at her cheeks. "I wish that hadn't been so hard. For either of us."

"Sometimes it takes broken souls a little longer. Though we fell in love pretty quickly." He chuckled. "You want to hear something funny?"

"Sure."

"I told my mother that I loved you when they were wheeling you out of this house and taking you to the hospital."

She gasped. "No way."

"I did. Oddly enough, everyone in my family already knew that. But I don't say those words to just anyone and I wanted to find the perfect time. I wanted it to be special because you're so very special to me. I can't imagine going through life without you in it. I was so scared you were going to die that night."

"But I didn't." She smiled.

"Nope, you didn't. And I love you and I'm going to keep telling you that. Over and over again. Because it rolls off my tongue like candy."

"Now you're being a dork." She leaned in, wincing a little, then kissing him softly.

"Does this mean you're going to make Lighthouse Cove your home?"

"I can't think of any other place I'd rather be." She smiled. "Or anyone else I'd rather be with."

And with that, Emmerson not only found his soulmate, but he mended every wound he'd held on to. Rumor was his lighthouse. His light, guiding him home.

His everything.

He'd love her until his last breath.

She was his to hold.

"You may kiss the bride."

Emmerson took his wife into his arms and placed a wet, passionate kiss on her sweet lips.

It had been a small ceremony at his mother's house. Family only. They hadn't wanted a big wedding. Nor had they wanted to take the time to plan one as they only got engaged two weeks ago. But neither one of them wanted to wait. They didn't see the point. Kind of like how Rumor never moved back into the pool house.

They fit together and their love for one another was as strong as ever.

"Yay, Uncle Emmerson!" his little niece Ally yelled.

A few more shouts and cheers erupted.

He was married.

To Rumor.

The woman who had captured his heart and become his partner. She was perfect and she looked beautiful in an ankle-length off-white dress with skinny straps that hugged her body.

"Save it for the honeymoon," his father shouted.

Reluctantly, he broke off the kiss and gazed into Rumor's adoring eyes. "Are you happy?"

"That is absolutely the dumbest question you have ever asked me."

He laughed. "Come on. Let's get a glass of champagne." He took his wife's hand and strolled proudly across the pool deck. A couple of his brothers slapped him on his back, congratulating him while a few of his nieces and nephews tossed confetti at him and his bride.

It was truly the single most joyous occasion of his life. He wasn't sure if life could get any better.

He stopped at the bar and lifted two flutes.

"Water for me," Rumor said. "I'm parched."

"Come on, babe. We need to celebrate. It's not every day I get married, and honestly, it won't ever happen again. You're it for me."

"I better be." She poked him in the chest.

"Ouch." He set one of the glasses down and handed her a water bottle.

His mother, father, and Steve approached. "He still hasn't figured it out yet, has he," his mother said with a smirk.

"Nope. For a smart man, sometimes he's as dumb as a doornail." Rumor twisted the cap off the water bottle and chugged.

"I take offense to that statement." He took a sip of champagne and glared at his parents, who smiled as if they harbored some giant secret.

Steve too.

Emmett sauntered over, carrying six-month-old Leslie. She stretched out her pudgy little arms, wiggling her fingers. "This one loves her uncle Emmerson."

"I love her right back." Emmerson took the little girl into his arms and blew raspberries on her cheek.

She full-on belly laughed, nuzzling her face in his neck. The final adoption papers had come through, and this little angel was officially the newest member of the family.

"You tell him yet?" Emmett asked.

"I've been playing the hinting game, but he hasn't figured it out," Rumor said.

"Seriously? What have you tried?" Emmett asked.

"I'm so lost in this conversation, it's beyond frustrating," Emmerson mumbled.

Rumor had become a member of the family long before he started shopping for an engagement ring. Her bond with his parents, his brothers and their wives and their children was unbreakable, and for that he was truly grateful. But sometimes, when they had their little private sidebars, it annoyed him, especially when it involved him.

"Well. Let's see. This morning it started with asking for crackers when we woke up." Rumor made a face at Leslie and tickled her belly. "Not only that, but I actually got sick."

"You were nervous," Emmerson said. "But I was a little worried she was getting cold feet."

"About marrying you? Are you nuts? I know a good thing when I see it." She shook her head. "Then I asked for flat soda. After that I bitched about how my dress was too tight and my boobs were getting bigger."

Emmerson sighed. "Can we please not talk about your girly parts with my family." He leaned closer. "And your boobs are fine. I didn't notice anything all that different."

"I better take this one back." Emmett took his daughter from Emmerson's hands. "Because when he does finally figure this out, he's either going to end up in the pool or on his ass. Either way, I don't want that happening with precious cargo in his arms."

"Oh my God. Would someone please tell me what the hell is going on? You all know I hate this kind of bullshit," Emmerson said. "Especially on my wedding day."

"Here's the best part. I left the test on the bathroom sink. He just threw it in the trash." Rumor took his hand and placed it on her stomach. "Without even asking me what it was. For a cop, and a detective, he wasn't being very observant."

"What test? What did I throw away?" The entire discussion had thrown Emmerson off-kilter.

"Jesus. I honestly can't believe you're my son," his father said.

"Really? Because four of seven times I had to practically beat you over the head with the concept." His mother planted her right hand on her hip and cocked her head.

"Four out of seven," Emmerson mumbled. "No champagne." He glanced from Rumor's smiling face with a single tear rolling down her cheek to his hand covering her belly. "Crackers. Soda. A long stick with a plus…" In a flash it all registered. A thick lump formed in his throat. "I think I need to sit down."

Steve shoved a stool under his ass.

"Oh, someone push him in the pool. He deserves it." Emmett walked away, laughing his ass off. His father followed.

"Come on, honey, let's give these two a little breathing room." Steve looped an arm around his mom and strolled across the pool deck.

"Are you okay?" Rumor eased between his legs, wrapping her arms around his shoulders.

He rested his hands on her hips, gripping on for dear life. He stared into her eyes and swallowed. Hard. Unable to form words.

"You did say you wanted to start a family," she said softly.

"I did," he managed to croak out.

"We agreed I'd go off birth control."

"That was only two months ago."

She smiled brightly. "And I'm about two months pregnant. Go figure."

He raised his hands, cupping her sweet, beautiful face. He would never tire of loving this woman. Ever. "A baby? We're going to have a baby?"

"Are you happy?"

"Now who's asking dumb questions." He kissed her in such a way that in the background, he heard some of the youngsters yell, "Ew, gross!"

"What a wedding present," he whispered. "And here, all I got you was a new car."

"At least you bought an SUV. That will come in handy when little Saucy is born." She cringed. "Yep. I heard that. Never again will I say it."

"I hope she has your eyes."

"I hope he has your sense of honor, but not your facial hair."

"Oh, that's mean." He kissed her nose. "I can't believe you told my entire family before me."

"For the record, that wasn't completely on purpose. I ran into your mother at the drugstore when I was buying the pregnancy test. She was with Trinity and Brie. It snowballed from there and I honestly thought you'd figure it out this morning. I hope you're not mad."

"Not even a little," he said. "I love you with everything I am and I will do my best to be a good father."

"You're going to be a great dad. It's me we need to worry about. Have you seen me try to change Leslie's diaper? What a mess."

"She's a little wiggle worm." Emmerson pulled his wife close, wrapping his arms tightly around the woman he loved. "You're going to be a wonderful mother."

"Emmerson?"

"Yes."

"You've made every fantasy I've ever dreamed about come true. I love you."

He would never get sick of hearing her say those words.

She was his to love.

His to cherish.

His to hold.

"Except one." She waggled her brows.

He covered her mouth. "Babe. I've done a few things with you against my better judgment. Sex in the patrol car, which if my mother knew, she'd fire me for it. Sex on the pool deck. We don't have a cage. Sex a few other places and some other things that has made this old man blush. But the handcuff thing is never going to happen as a matter of principle, so stop asking." Only, he was warming to the idea.

Thank you for reading MINE TO HOLD. Please feel free to leave an honest review. Next up in the series is **Mine to Love.**

Grab a glass of vino, kick back, relax, and let the romance roll in…

Sign up for my Newsletter (https://dl.bookfunnel.com/82gm8b9k4y) where I often give away free books before publication.

Join my private Facebook group (https://www.facebook.com/groups/191706547909047/) where I post exclusive excerpts and discuss all things murder and love!

ABOUT THE AUTHOR

Jen Talty is the *USA Today* Bestselling Author of Contemporary Romance, Romantic Suspense, and Paranormal Romance. In the fall of 2020, her short story was selected and featured in a 1001 Dark Nights Anthology.

Regardless of the genre, her goal is to take you on a ride that will leave you floating under the sun with warmth in your heart. She writes stories about broken heroes and heroines who aren't necessarily looking for romance, but in the end, they find the kind of love books are written about :).

She first started writing while carting her kids to one hockey rink after the other, averaging 170 games per year between 3 kids in 2 countries and 5 states. Her first book, IN TWO WEEKS was originally published in 2007. In 2010 she helped form a publishing company (Cool Gus Publishing) with *NY Times* Bestselling Author Bob Mayer where she ran the technical side of the business through 2016.

Jen is currently enjoying the next phase of her life… the empty nester! She and her husband reside in Jupiter, Florida.

Grab a glass of vino, kick back, relax, and let the romance roll in…

Sign up for my Newsletter (https://dl.bookfunnel.com/ 82gm8b9k4y) where I often give away free books before publication.

Join my private Facebook group (https://www.facebook.com/ groups/191706547909047/) where I post exclusive excerpts and discuss all things murder and love!

Never miss a new release. Follow me on Amazon:amazon.com/author/jentalty

And on Bookbub: bookbub.com/authors/jen-talty

Brand new series: SAFE HARBOR!

Mine To Keep

Mine To Save

Mine To Protect

Mine to Hold

Mine to Love

Check out LOVE IN THE ADIRONDACKS!

Shattered Dreams

An Inconvenient Flame

The Wedding Driver

Clear Blue Sky

Blue Moon

Before the Storm

NY STATE TROOPER SERIES (also set in the Adirondacks!)

In Two Weeks

Dark Water

Deadly Secrets

Murder in Paradise Bay

To Protect His own

Deadly Seduction

When A Stranger Calls

His Deadly Past

The Corkscrew Killer

First Responders: A spin-off from the NY State Troopers series

Playing With Fire

Private Conversation

The Right Groom

After The Fire

Caught In The Flames

Chasing The Fire

Legacy Series

Dark Legacy

Legacy of Lies

Secret Legacy

Emerald City

Investigate Away

Sail Away

Fly Away

Flirt Away

Colorado Brotherhood Protectors

Fighting For Esme

Defending Raven

Fay's Six

Darius' Promise

Yellowstone Brotherhood Protectors

Guarding Payton

Wyatt's Mission

Corbin's Mission

Candlewood Falls

Rivers Edge

The Buried Secret

Its In His Kiss

Lips Of An Angel

Kisses Sweeter than Wine

A Little Bit Whiskey

It's all in the Whiskey

Johnnie Walker

Georgia Moon

Jack Daniels

Jim Beam

Whiskey Sour

Whiskey Cobbler

Whiskey Smash

Irish Whiskey

The Monroes

Color Me Yours

Color Me Smart

Color Me Free

Color Me Lucky

Color Me Ice

Color Me Home

Search and Rescue

Protecting Ainsley

Protecting Clover

Protecting Olympia

Protecting Freedom

Protecting Princess

Protecting Marlowe

Fallport Rescue Operations

Searching for Madison

Searching for Haven

DELTA FORCE-NEXT GENERATION

Shielding Jolene

Shielding Aalyiah

Shielding Laine

Shielding Talullah

Shielding Maribel

Shielding Daisy

The Men of Thief Lake

Rekindled

Destiny's Dream

Federal Investigators

Jane Doe's Return

The Butterfly Murders

THE AEGIS NETWORK

The Sarich Brother

The Lighthouse

Her Last Hope

The Last Flight

The Return Home

The Matriarch

Aegis Network: Jacksonville Division

A SEAL's Honor

Aegis Network Short Stories

Max & Milian

A Christmas Miracle

Spinning Wheels

Holiday's Vacation

Special Forces Operation Alpha

Burning Desire

Burning Kiss

Burning Skies

Burning Lies

Burning Heart

Burning Bed

Remember Me Always

The Brotherhood Protectors

Out of the Wild

Rough Justice

Rough Around The Edges

Rough Ride

Rough Edge

Rough Beauty

The Brotherhood Protectors

The Saving Series

Saving Love

Saving Magnolia

Saving Leather

Hot Hunks

Cove's Blind Date Blows Up

My Everyday Hero – Ledger

Tempting Tavor

Malachi's Mystic Assignment

Needing Neor

Holiday Romances

A Christmas Getaway

Alaskan Christmas

Whispers

Christmas In The Sand

Heroes & Heroines on the Field

Taking A Risk

Tee Time

A New Dawn

The Blind Date

Spring Fling

Summers Gone

Winter Wedding

The Awakening

The Collective Order

The Lost Sister

The Lost Soldier

The Lost Soul

The Lost Connection

The New Order